SINFUL WORDS

HESENÊ METÊ

Translated from Kurdish by
Sabahat Karaduman

authorHOUSE®

AuthorHouse™ UK
1663 Liberty Drive
Bloomington, IN 47403 USA
www.authorhouse.co.uk
Phone: 0800.197.4150

Published by AuthorHouse 06/17/2017

ISBN: 978-1-5246-8252-1 (sc)
ISBN: 978-1-5246-8253-8 (e)

And now you ask me what happened after. In my maturity, I am not going to dishonour myself in the face of God, nor the Great Emir, nor yourselves. No, really, I am not going to do that. I am not going to line up the words and make the story long. If you did not have this gate in front of you now – the gate that you are going to enter or have already entered – I would not have to tell you the story.

It is not important to me at all who you are and what you are, and what race or nationality you are. And you don't get to ask me who I am, what I am, and where I come from because in the mysterious existence of human beings, labels have no importance. The important thing is to know that there is a door at the present and in the world where we live – a door that leads to a world we live off and fooled off – and we believe there is such a door and have faith in it. Some believe that it is the wonder of God. Others call it God's will. I leave it to you and to your belief. I leave it to you and to your understanding. Let me tell you the story...

When I found myself in that holy place – but do not ask me what holy place because I do not know it myself- It was such a place, how I can put it in words? A place I will never forget, I keep coming back to it. Wherever I go, I return to this place.

Whatever roofless barns in the open at night mean to resting herds, this place has a similar meaning to me. It gives me peace of mind and makes me relax. But I cannot tell you where it is. Even to me, it sounds like a nowhere place, a hidden place that is clean and far from lies, pain, and evil. A virgin place that is free from sin. Only peace of mind reposes there. In other words, there is only one truth – the reality of me and the reality of God. There I am nobody, nothing but myself.

If I had a poetic spirit, I would tell you that this place feels like your mother's breast. Think about your childhood for a moment. Lie on your mother's lap. Put your head on her breasts, which are full of pure white milk, and doze off to a peaceful sleep. That is what this place feels like.

If you want to come, just follow me there. It does not exist around here, for everything stays still there. Everything stands still there; ants stand still, children stand still and God stands still there.

What do you think? OK, let me tell you again.

Back at that time, in my childhood, I thought and I had a feeling that God created me so that I would love him just for himself. And I did love him, right up to my maturity and years of discretion. Like a confident Jew, I stood up for God and laid claim to him. I liked him as a Christian does. I prayed like a devout Muslim in prayer time for God. I acted in every era of those religions. Now, when I look back and think about it, believe me, I knew even back then that God is like a child. If you don't like him, he will be offended. He will get upset and annoyed with you, and he will drift away.

In other words, I sought him for a long time. With every step and every breath I took, I looked for His Excellency God.

What was I telling you? Ah yes. In those days, I was a student at the faculty of theology in the town of 'E'. The new term had just started. A month before I started, I rented the house I lived in from a gentleman. No offence to anyone, but he was a real gentleman who had given himself entirely to God. A pious man. As a matter of fact, we got to know each other because of God and in the house of God. In other words, God was aware of our meeting. This mutual path was what got the two of us together at the mosque.

In the town of E, at the house of God, right in the middle of the noon *salaat* I was turning my head to my left to give the angels the final greeting, and our eyes met. That was how we got to know each other.

He was a clean-faced, kind-looking, fit, polite, middle-aged gentleman. As I said, he looked like a real friend of God in his appearance and attitude. Perhaps that is why I liked him and felt close to him. He also seemed pleased with my piety.

After turning his head first to the right and then to the left, giving final greetings to the angels, and mumbling the prophet Muhammad's name, he turned to me and said, 'May God accept your prayers. May God help us to keep our faith.'

'Amen,' I replied.

Still kneeling and trying to correct my posture, I continued, 'Worshipping Allah and praying to him is very delicate. It is just like the eggs under a broody hen. If the hen moves away from the eggs too early, before it is mature, the eggs will go cold and become useless.'

I am not sure whether my words impressed him. He answered me with a saintly smile while he also tried, like I did, to improve his sitting position. 'May God give you a long life, young man. You are right. You cannot rush through a prayer. There should be no rush when praying. May I ask your name, young man? Where are you from?'

It was obvious that he wanted to know about the part of this town I was from. 'I am not from this town, Uncle. My name is Behram.'

'May you live long, Behram. But what city are you from?'

'I am from the east, from Kawash in Van, Uncle.'

4

Hearing the name Kawash put a sweet smile on the gentleman's face. He was plunged into thought for a while, and then he looked at me. With a wide smile, he said, 'I had a friend called Kinyaz, whom I did my national service with. He was also from Kawash. He was from Birîma tribe. We used to call him Kinyazê Birîmî – Kinyaz from Birîm. He had a soft way of talking and a pleasant manner. He was a kind-hearted man but just a little bit rebellious. His rebelliousness made him unforgettable. He once stood up to the commander. He did not obey the rules, and we all had to suffer as a result. We were beaten repeatedly on our hands and feet. Then we were punished for three days with isolation and had to survive on only bread and water. That was Kinyaz, the rebel. No offence meant, but he was also from Kawash.'

I don't know why, but I turned around, and with a smile like his, answered, 'As a matter of fact, disobedience started in Kawash, Uncle. The ancient garden of Eden was in today's Kawash. As you know, the disobedience of Adam and Eve happened there. In other words, disobedience has its origin in Kawash and has spread all over the world from there.'

After those words of mine, his face changed from happiness to curiosity, as if he heard something new. 'May God bless you, Behram! Really? Is that true? Was the garden of Eden there in Kawash?'

'So they say.'

He spoke in a curious and suspicious way, as if my answer was not satisfying enough. 'So God has created his comrade, His Excellency Prophet Adam, out of the sacred earth and holy mud in Kawash, and God's gardens of heaven are there in Kawash. Is that what you are saying?'

5

'Only God knows where his heavenly paradise is. But according to religious wise men and theologists, and according to holy books and ancient signs, it seems that Kawash is the site of Eden,' I replied.

In the mosque and outside in the yard, we kept talking a while about this holy subject, about God, his land, and his creatures. As if I was one of those creatures from that sacred place, the garden of Eden, he asked me why I was in E. When I told him I was going to study at the school of theology and looking for somewhere to rent, he told me he had a house in the city that was empty, and I could rent it from him.

After our meeting at God's house, we walked together to his house in one of the old quarters of the city. He showed me his house, and we reached an agreement right there and then. The gentleman gave me the key, and I officially became his tenant.

A short time after the beginning of the term, we ran into each other in the city. My landlord was Lulu Khan. For yes, this is what his name is – Lulu Khan. I paid him rent for the three autumn months in advance. I told him about myself, my well-being, and about the comfort of the house. I showed him my gratitude, and though he did not tell me verbally, I could see he was happy with me, too.

Besides our mutual affection, I liked his attitude: the way he avoided counting the rent money like shrewd countrymen when I handed it to him. He didn't have the cheap civil service mentality checking the walls, looking for damages inch by inch. In addition, he did not forbid me to hammer any pins in the wall.

He invited me to his place. He asked me to go and visit him and his family in his village and stay with them the next weekend. He told me that I can bring some grapes and figs back with me to the city. Then he started talking about the village, the woods, the waters, the vineyards, and the gardens and greens around his place. He talked about the life in the village and described it as a cool, green, and marshy area. He then explained which bus to take and how to get to his home.

So I decided to go.

It is mid autumn, and the day is Saturday. The chilliness of the morning has softened, and the time is near noon.

I take the bus as my landlord Lulu Khan advised me and head towards the south. After a short journey – the length of two smoked cigarettes – I arrive at the village called Argon.

Argon is in the skirt of a difficult mountain near the road. The village is full of trees and has natural springs. The water originates from the mountain to the north. It looks as if the mountain protects the village from the cold winds, storms, and any harm coming from that direction. The mountain is covered with trees from the foothill up to the top, and they have already dressed up with the autumn's yellow and reddish colours.

Lulu Khan, lives in this village. By asking various locals, and with help from two small children, I walk through the village to its upper side. The children show me a building that is a sling's throw away from the village on the upper end. The building, which is lying on the southeast of a vineyard, looks like a big, white castle between all the trees. The green of the vineyards stretches from the castle to embrace the lower slopes of the mountain.

I head towards the castle and reach the gate. It is on two floors and is surrounded by fig and pomegranate trees. The outer walls of the building are so white that it makes me believe that it has been built in dedication to God. The building is so different in every way from the ones in the village below. I say different because it looks as if it is not built from this soil and that it is not from this village's inhabitants. It doesn't look as if the house and the rest belong together. As I said before, the castle is away from the houses and it is outside the village.

It gives more the impression of a holy monastery than a big house or a castle. It makes me think that Lulu Khan has distanced himself from the wickedness and goodness of his fellow countrymen and has built his castle outside and away from the village so that he can pray and worship in peace and quietness, away from the problems of the village inhabitants. That is what I think.

In front of the gate, I catch the sight of my landlord, Lulu Khan. He is sitting with a lady on the *sekûk*[1], and they are sunning their faces and taking it easy.

'Good day, and may God give you a healthy life and luck!'

With my greeting, they look up and see me. They both stand up and walk towards me by the gate. With a smile on his face, Lulu Khan greets me with God's words, shakes my hand, offers me a stool with low legs like the ones in the madrasa and says:

'You are very welcome, Behram. We were waiting for you with God's mercy. I told the family that you were coming. Please come up on the sekûk and rest a little bit.'

He turns towards the woman and continues.

---

[1] A wide, raised bench of earth.

'And this lady, she is my *halal* spouse.'[2]

The halal spouse is standing roughly three steps behind him with a long string of prayer bead made of olive stones in her hand. She comes closer to me and gives me a warm greeting as if she already knows me well.

My landlord, Lulu Khan, turns to his wife and says over and over again:

'It is him, Lady Geshtina. Behram, this is the young man from Kawash, the one I told you about. He is one of God's wise men. May God bless him! He is truly knowledgeable about theology. Please, Lady Geshtina, go and get him a glass of cold water from the well.'

I am not used to being complimented and praised. Those words of Lulu Khan make the sweat run on my body, but I still act like an omniscient theologian and step onto the sekûk in the garden and sit on the stool. The garden looks big with its walls, trees, and the well.

Lady Geshtina brings me cold water from the tap on the well. After quenching my thirst with the cold water, Lulu Khan and his wife and I all sit down.

It is obvious from the white, two-story house with its big garden that they are well off. The cleanness and the layout of the garden, the whiteness of the walls, and especially the embroideries and patterns around the wide window frames all show that it has been touched by talented hands.

While sitting on the sekûk, without asking me whether I am hungry, Lady Geshtina stands up, goes into the house, and comes back out with some food to eat on a copper tray. She puts it in front of me and says:

---

[2] He means religiously legitimate spouse.

'Please, help yourself, my dear. It is just whatever was ready at home to eat. Please make yourself at home and eat.'

When they join me and with their company, I do indeed feel at home, and we all start eating together. Both during and after the meal, they enthusiastically ask me questions about my education. They sincerely wish me good luck with my studies and good health. Their happiness about my devoting myself to God's way and to studying theology is obvious in their faces, in their behaviour, and in their talk. As if he wants to show me his enthusiasm, Lulu Khan turns to me and says:

'May God be with you, Behram! May God not turn you away from the right way. May God make your belief and faith stronger, and he will inshallah. Not everyone is lucky enough to be able to dive that deep and swim far in the faith of God as you do. We ourselves have two children. No offense to you, but they are lovely children. May God be happy with them as we are happy with them, and may God show them the right way. They have no higher education. They only finished junior school in the village, and they remained here. May God prevent everyone, even our children, from weakening of belief and faith.'

'Amen,' I reply, and then I ask them about their current life and work. They tell me that it is harvest time for the grapes. They explain how they pick up the grapes, how to make the grape juice, and how to boil the juice. Whilst he is in the middle of telling me the procedure for handling grapes, the thought suddenly enters my head that their children are grown up, married, and moved from home. It seems to me that these two aged people of God are living on their own in this house. They sit next to each other day

and night, trying to put their love and strength together to
get closer to God. Unable to control my curiosity, I interrupt
and I ask Lulu Khan:

'You mentioned two children, but you did not say
whether you live together or they have moved out and live
far away from you. Who is doing all the jobs and house
chores?'

Lulu Khan turns towards me and answers with a smile.

'We and the twins live together. Our children are twins.
They are in the vineyard right now and are busy cleaning
the basin and galleys. They prepare for the harvest of the
grapes that needs being put in the basin and be squashed
for the grape juice. Our children are grown up and they are
at the age of marriage, so they are doing most of the chores.
The jobs that cannot manage by ourselves are done by the
people from the village, thank heavens! They get paid for the
jobs, God bless them. Even the sheep and cattle are looked
after by the villagers.'

While listening to him, I am looking around with
curiosity. I look at the outdoor tap on the well, at the
garden wall, and at the fig trees with its branches hanging
and covering the garden wall. I look at the building, the
embroideries, and the patterns around the windows and on
window frames – two big windows. When I look at those
embroideries around the windows, I suddenly see something
that looks like an edge of a big aluminium bowl on the eaves
at the top of the window. It is either shining, or something
is gliding. I am not sure. It catches my attention, but at
first, I cannot understand what it is. It looks to me like a
piece of metal shining under the glare of the sun. I try not
to distract my hosts by drawing their attention to what has

caught my eye, so I ask about the patterns and their origin.
Lady Geshtina answers my question.

'I don't know. I do not know what the patterns mean
and where she has her inspiration. Our daughter Nagina has
painted them. I think she used the colours of wool rugs, of
kilim.'

The embroideries and patterns look old, as if they
belong to a past era. They are like symbols with hidden
meaning. They catch my imagination. I don't say anything
to the old couple, but I think for myself: their daughter is
not educated, yet look at all those embroideries and patterns!
Yes! Yes, they are old-time surrealistic dream patterns.

All three of us look at those embroideries and patterns
above the window simultaneously. We look with such a
curiosity and carefulness as if each of us wants to gain
something from them. At that moment, I again see
something that looks like the edge of a big aluminium bowl.
It is gliding along the eaves of the house. I raise my voice.

'Look! Oh God! There is a snake in the eaves of your
house.'

I jump out of my seat without meaning to. I rush round
looking for something to bring the snake down with. I look
anxiously and apprehensively at Lulu Khan, silently wishing
that he could bring a gun, a stick, or a cudgel to kill the
snake with and bring it down. I feel it is my duty to kill
the snake because my landlords are too old for that kind of
choires. It seems to be my duty to find a stick or a stone. I
look around me in a great agitation.

Before Lulu Khan even manages to say something, Lady
Geshtina stretches her hand towards me as if begging. She
talks fast as if a stone has got caught in her throat.

'No, my dear, no! It would be a pity. Calm down. Sit! That snake is not hurting anyone. It is a house snake.'

It is the first time I have heard of a 'house snake'. Yet Lady Geshtina mentions it in such a simple matter-of-fact way that it sounds like a common thing to have a house snake. But I read a hidden worry and fear in her face. I realise straight away that she is afraid I may try to kill the snake. She doesn't want me to kill it or do anything at all. She gets up slowly, fetches a piece of cloth, and sets light to it. She then places the cloth on a piece of dried manure, holds the manure as a holy smoke and lifts it high up towards the eaves. The smoke from the cloth on the dried manure travels up to the eaves towards the stomach of the snake and then billows out. During the ceremony, she murmurs as if she is calming a pet dog. She does it quietly first and then she starts singing loudly.

> *Marê martîze*
> *ev dem êdî payiz e*
> *ne guhdar ke ne bibihîze*
> *tu bide xatirê Mîrê xwe î mezin*
> *û here ji vir dûr bilîze!*[3]

Lady Geshtina's song and approach calms me down a little bit, but I cannot stop silently laughing at this country folk behaviour. Their way of life seems so simple and sweet

---

[3] Oh snake of the snake origin,
The time is autumn.
Neither listen to what is said nor hear it
For the sake of the Great Lord.
Go away from here and play somewhere far away.

to me. I pull my stool away from the eaves and sit down. To be honest, I feel stunned and a bit disappointed that they didn't listen to me and allow me to kill the snake and pull it down. My eyes are on the eaves of the house while I talk about the evil and the enmity of snakes from holy verses and books.

'He is God's enemy. God has said in all holy books and told the snake directly: "Because you have done this, you are cursed more than all cattle and every beast of the field. You will go flat on the earth, and dust will be your food all the days of your life: And there will be war between you and the woman and between your seed and her seed: by him will your head be crushed and by you his foot will wounded."[4]
'So has the evil snake remained until now; it has remained as God's enemy.'

Lulu Khan lifts his head up towards the eaves of the house and looks once again at the enemy of God. He gets blinded by the beams of the sun. He turns his head to the other side and he sneezes: 'Achoo ... achooo!'

His wife, Lady Geshtina, with praying beads in her hand turns to him with blessing eyes and says, 'Bless you!'

Lulu Khan wipes his mouth and lips with the back of his sleeve.

'Thank you, may God bless your father's dead soul,' he says. He adjusts his sitting position on the stool, turns to his wife, and continues with a sigh.

'Yes, Lady Geshtina. Come on, tell once again the story of your father so that this nice young man, Behram, can also hear it.'

---

[4] Bible: Genesis 3:14, 15

He proudly turns his head towards me so that I listen carefully to the story his wife is going to tell of his father-in-law. He tells about the incident.

'It is such an unusual incident that people still call it a mystery. It has become a legend that everyone knows and interprets in their own way. Let Lady Geshtina tell you about it now while you listen. It is an absolutely divine incident.'

I am listening to Lulu Khan, but my attention is still at the edge of the eaves because of my fear of the snake. I see that the snake is now slithering away, and then it disappears. According to Lady Geshtina, the house snake is going from here and will play somewhere far away for the sake of the great Emir.

Lulu Khan looks at me like a wise savant and points his hand up to the eaves of the roof with a smile on his face and says:

'You were talking about enmity and killing that holy snake. That is how I remembered the story about the incident, Behram. You just listen to it.'

As if he wants his wife to start telling the story at once, he kind of winds her up by adding:

'O dear God! Mekrus effendi must have been such a good man and a real man of God! It seems as if he was a saint.'

My curiosity begins to increase about the story. Lady Geshtina – in other words, the daughter of Mekrus Effendi, the daughter of the saint – sighs deeply as if in confirmation of her husband's words. She starts to tell the story slowly.

These are the words of Lady Geshtina.

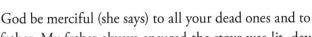

God be merciful (she says) to all your dead ones and to my father. My father always ensured the stove was lit, day and night, twenty-four hours a day, seven days a week, the whole year of God. I remember well: Late at night, when the fire was nearly out, he would always cover the last few glowing coals with ashes to keep it alive. He would say: 'The fire must always be kept alive'. I don't know why he would say that and keep the fire alive.

My dad was on his own most of the time. He was like that even in his childhood. He was on his own round here and in the village. As far as I remember and know, he was on his own in his soul and in his own world – only him. It was as if he wanted to get used to the loneliness of the other side, in life after death, as if he preferred to be lonely. He did not want anyone to share his loneliness. Most of the time it felt like there was no place for his words on this planet. He hid his words inside himself, and he would not talk. I mean he would rarely talk. Why am I telling you about his character?

Yes, he had a very special world of his own. But my father was an unpretentious person, and he would not say anything bad or evil. Bad behaviour, jealousy, mischief, and intrigue were strangers to his personality. He liked everyone. He liked everyone and everything created so abundantly by God. But there is a saying: 'There is no wheat field without couch grass'. This incident is something like that.

Our house was in the village in those days. I don't know why, but even then my father wanted to build this house here in the middle of the vineyards and to dig a well in the garden. It is this well here. The incident happened in the process of digging the well. My father had paid two of his friends to help him. My parents were newly married at that time, and I was not yet born. I still do not know who those friends of my father were. After the incident, my father had told my mother not to tell anyone. 'It is better that no one knows. There is no good in people knowing such things.' That is what my father had told my mum. He did not tell me, either, when I had grown up. He would talk about the incident. He used to tell me the story, but he would not mention the names of those two friends.

My father and his friends had dug the well to the height of a man. He then told them: 'I will go down in the well and dig, and you two will lift up and carry away the soil with the buckets.' They had continued to dig for fifteen days to the length of a *weris*[5] and the depth of a few hands when my father noticed that the soil started to be very soft. It was so soft that it felt like rotted compost. My father kept digging in hope of reaching water.

---

[5] A rope of roughly three and a half meter.

He told me that it was one of those digging days again when he was working deep down in the well and his friends were working together above well. He suddenly got a strange feeling as if a worm was crawling inside his brain, and something told him to look up at the wall at the level of his head. May his soul rest in peace. He used to say: 'I felt as if I heard a voice telling me to look up.' So he did. He looked at the wall and saw something that resembled the handle of an earthenware jug. When he reached down to the handle, a whole earthenware pitcher slid into his hand. He stiffened with surprise. He remained in that position for a while. He told me that it came up as easily as if someone had simply handed him the pitcher. The weight of the jug told him that it was full. The bottom of the well was in semi-darkness but he could see that the top of the jug was covered with something like wax.

When my deceased, blessed father removed the wax, he saw that it was full of gold coins. Immediately, he tied the rope around his waist and he signalled to his friends to pull him up. He told his friends about his discovery and he emptied the whole jug on the ground in front of them. He then counted the coins one by one. There were three hundred and sixty gold coins, all of them identical. My father then gave each of his friends one twelfth of the treasure as a kind gesture and then returned to the bottom of the well and continued to dig. After a while he reached the water table, but he still kept digging until it was impossible to continue digging because there was too much water. My father then gave his friends the good news about the water and asked them to pull him up again, which they did.

The story goes that my father suggested they would have a break to eat, smoke, and rest before they placed big stones at the base of the well and the walls to secure and stabilise everything. They all washed their hands and faces in preparation for the meal. The food was placed in the shadow of the drystone garden wall. The drystone wall was then here instead of this current wall. My father used to tell me that my mother placed a big tray with *sîrmastik*[6], a plunger full of natural yogurt, egg omelette, fresh bread, and spring onions for lunch by the drystone wall in the shadow.

Before my dad could invite his friends to go sit down to eat, they saw a spotted red snake that suddenly slithered out of a hole in the drystone wall and stretched itself towards the plunger full of yogurt. As I said before, that wall was exactly here, where this new wall is placed. My deceased blessed father used to say: 'The spots were as beautiful as if they were painted by hand'. May he rest in peace. He would then quickly correct himself with a smile and say: 'No, such beautiful patterns have not been drawn by descendants of Adam. Such a beautiful rope of various coloured strands has not been twisted together yet. Those patterns have never been created by talented hands of ladies in the woven matting workshops. Those patterns are the masterwork of God.' He made it clear that he was amazed by the patterns, that he was stunned and speechless and just wanted to watch the snake. He was telling me from his heart: 'That snake was looking at me as if I was the only person that mattered. He was smiling only at me. It felt as if those eyes were familiar to me, that we knew each other from somewhere.'

---

[6] Chunks of pita bread covered with garlic yogurt with melted butter and chilli sauce on the top.

He said all this happened in an instant. My father's friends – as I said, I still do not know who they are – as soon as they saw the snake, they grabbed wooden sticks and stones to attack it. But the spell of the snake had amazed my father so much that he hastily put his hands on the friends' shoulders and cried: 'Leave him! Leave him alone to have his share of food. One must not touch a snake whilst it is eating or drinking.'

They left the snake alone after those words, but they kept looking at it with dread and evil eyes. The red-spotted snake bent his head to the plunger filled with yoghurt and started eating. Then he lifted his head and looked at them as if to say 'Don't be disloyal'. The second time he put his head in the plunger he stayed longer. When the snake lifted his head this time, he started shivering. He looked again at my father and his friends. My father used to swear to God that the holy snake was meaningfully looking at us as if it was saying 'You traitors are not reliable'.

And the third time he stretched his head to the plunger, he kind of coughed with his mouth shut and then vomited and emptied his whole stomach in the plunger. My father said: 'I don't get it. When the snake turned around and started disappearing between the stones in the wall, he was not as quick or strong as he was before. It was like as if he was numb or had pins and needles and he was not as fit.'

Later – a long time later – those friends of my father told people in a roundabout way that they both agreed that one of them – God knows which one of the two – went away quickly to fetch flea poison and mixed it in the yoghurt in the plunger. They were going to let my father eat first, and God knows what else they had been thinking. But my father was such a man he did not mention who those two friends were till he died. I still do not know. Even though he loved me so much, he did not tell even me. He didn't have a habit of talking too much anyway. Sometimes he would not talk for days.

As a matter of fact, he never told anyone about the ending of the story, the part about his friends mixing the flea poison with the yoghurt. Later, after his death, I heard about it from others. My father didn't care about those things. I think he shut his ears to the gossip and did not want to hear it. I think he believed that human beings are created to be traitors and such behaviour is not so unfamiliar for Adam's descendants.

According to his peers, my father was like that since his childhood. He liked the snakes from his childhood. He used to catch them with his hands, play with them, enjoy them, and then let them go again. According to some people – those who are good at exaggerating things – according to them, my father could even talk the snake language.

After that incident, my father's attitude and feelings towards snakes became much more marked. He would clearly and openly tell everybody: 'No, there is no such thing. It is not possible that such a delicate, slender and sweet creature as a snake is the symbol for badness or wickedness. Snakes are not for killing. They have got something very mysteriously holy in their soul, but not everybody is able to see that.'

People would look at him in shock and amazement, saying: 'Don't say that, Mekrus effendi; don't commit a sin. It is a religious duty and necessity to kill snakes. It says so in all the holy verses and tales. It is even a command from God.'

Anyway, I don't know. Only God knows, but my father used to insist that his opinion was right whenever there was talk about snakes. May all the dead ones rest in peace, he as well. I remember that whenever he heard that someone had killed a snake, he would get very upset. He felt the pain as if one of his fingers had been chopped off. In those situations, people would be more persistent with him and say to him:

'Your behaviour is rebellious Mekrus effendi. It is a denial of and a rebellion against God. The snake misled our mother, Eve, and led her astray. God has legitimated killing snakes and has even made it a good act of conduct on earth.'

They would say many other things. I remember well that they used to bring their holy books with them, put them in front of my father, turn page after page, and read word for word the words of God to try to convince him otherwise. During those loud arguments, sometimes I would hear them say:

'Now, despite all those words of God, how dare you still say that snakes should not be killed, Mekrus effendi?'

My father would not answer the questions. He would simply smile and would still insist in what he believed. His persistence made some people question his religious beliefs and become wary and suspicious of his devotion.

Without saying anything bad or good, I listen to the stories of Mekrus effendi with suspicion, in amazement, and with curiosity. Lady Geshtina stops. There is silence for a while. Then she looks at me and puts an end to the story of her father with her simple and pure way of talking when she sees and realises that I listen carefully to what she says.

'Yes, that was my father's story. As I said, when the snake vomited in the plunger, my father poured the yoghurt out and he and his friends ate the remaining food on the tray, which was untouched. My poor father could have been killed by flea poison for the sake of gold coins – worldly goods that you cannot take with you when you die. Now tell me, how could someone do such spiteful harm? The blessed soul has already given you your share! Haven't you ever heard the words of God? Was it not the fear of God that turned you all into sinners?'

It is obvious to me that Lady Geshtina was moved by the story she told, and it made her upset. Those last words of hers were full of reproach for those sinful people as if they were standing in front of her right then – those sinful men who tried to poison her father for the sake of gold coins.

She does not raise her hands up and curse the sinful men, but she looks up at the sky as if she was asking all the angels for help to endure the pain.

Just to say something or perhaps in an effort to share her dejection and make her feel better, I say:

'I understand, Lady Geshtina. One becomes disappointed and sad over how human beings can plan such awful deeds for the sake of worldly goods. What kind of soul is inside a body filled with such wickedness? God has placed such a clear and clean soul inside the ribcage of a human body where there is more than enough space for all the words of God. But despite all the words of soundness, words of kindness and goodness that have been sent down by his angels, there are still people around who have not got any of that goodness. They have no space left in their hearts for any of the angels' words.

'It seems that both of Mekrus effendi's friends were two such people. Such weak souls are easily influenced by the Devil. When the Devil finds he cannot steal a man's soul, he tries to overpower him with the lure of worldly goods. It looks like the Devil succeeded in misleading the friends of your father with worldly goods. The Devil, it seems, succeeded in overpowering their weak souls. May God reform them and put them on the right track for they have sinned. They have been riding on the Devil's horse and acted as the Devil wanted. They have accepted the wickedness as a job. They wanted to feed themselves with evil and live with the sins.

'It has been said – it is a myth of course – that Malik bin Dinar, when asked "How are you?" answered by saying: "I am doing well. I listen to the Devil and live on God's good benefaction. I am fine".

'Sinful people were around yesterday and are still around today. There is no shortage of them. You can come across them and meet them everywhere. May God not be displeasured and get annoyed, but it is already known that people like that will never make it to the gate of the Lord's heaven. They will have to face the truth one day.'

Lady Geshtina is quiet after my words. I am not sure whether my words have aired her soul or made her feel relieved, but I can see that Lulu Khan is shaking his head up and down in rhythm with every sentence I say as if they are words of a holy book, and I witness his happiness. He puts his happiness into words and says:

'God bless you, Behram! May God keep everyone on the right way! May God save everyone from leaving the path of righteousness! May God put those ones on the wrong path back on the right way, clean, and purify their weakened and wicked souls!'

'Amen,' I say, and I can see their pure and clean souls. In order to keep their souls clean against badness and wickedness forever, I tell them a religious myth. I do not remember now where I had heard it.

'Once upon a time, on a full moon night, the Prophet Muhammad went to visit the Kaaba. The Prophet met Ebu Cehil and a group of some tribes. Ebu Cehil was tense and troubled that the Prophet would show off with some kind of enchanting magic. He then put two pieces of gravel in his hand and hid them. He walked towards the Prophet and said: "If you are not going to cheat or do witchcraft again, and if you really are getting your power from your God, then tell me what I have got in my hand. Come on, tell me!"

'Right at that moment, Gabriel the archangel came to the Prophet's help and whispered in his ear what to tell that hypocrite.

'The Prophet said: "Do you want me to tell you, or do you want the things in your hands to tell you what they are?"

'Ebu Cehil started shivering, but he still insisted on getting an answer. "The last one is better," he said.

'Immediately, the two pieces of gravel began to talk. Despite this, Ebu Cehil was still not convinced. He said: "There is always an empty hole —a way to cheat on this earth. There is the high sky, and we all know you cannot reach it. If what you do is not cheating and is divine wisdom, then separate the full moon into two pieces in the sky."

'Gabriel the archangel came to the Prophet's help once again and told him what to do. The Prophet lifted his hand up towards the moon in the sky, mumbled the name of God, parted his fingers, and said: "The Hour has come near, and the moon has split in two."[7]

'According to the myth, at that moment the moon divided in two pieces and the whole planet was surrounded by a strange sound. All the cattle, the flocks, and herds died. Many of the people who lived in the deserts caught unnamed diseases and died. Those who had feared this divine wisdom and power began to believe in God. They all came to the Prophet Muhammad and piteously implored him to put the two pieces of the moon back together again. And so His Excellency did this by saying God's name and raising his holy fingers. Yes, he put the two pieces of the

---

[7] Quran: Surah The moon / al Qamar 54:1.

divided moon back into one whole piece like a white, round tortilla wrap.

'But Ebu Cehil remained stubborn, as was his nature, and refused to be converted to the true faith. For even at those times there were wicked people like Ebu Cehil, those without faith. That is perhaps why the following holy words have been sent down to us: "But as for those in whose hearts is sickness: it adds disgrace to their disgrace, and they die as unbelievers."[8]

'Our conversation about the clean and muddied souls reminded me of this myth. May God keep the clean souls away from the evil ones! It seems that every era has its own specific evilness and goodness. But God sees and knows everything. God provides hindrances and barriers to prevent wickedness in a way that is difficult to imagine. The work of God is such a thing that human beings are unable to grasp it. This is exactly what has happened in the case of your father, Mekrus effendi, a holy and magical miracle. Think about it: God provided the snake to prevent a bad and evil soul from performing its evilness.'

That is what I tell them, and I understand better now why Lady Geshtina called the snake a 'house snake' and did not let me kill it. I see and understand from their facial expressions and their behaviour that they see me as one of them, a family member, and they enjoy my company and our conversations.

Lady Geshtina lowers her head and her eyes and says:

'*Amentubillah*[9] The work of God is wondrous. May God be merciful to all the dead ones' souls, and the soul of my

---

[8] Quran: Surah Repetance / al Tawbah 9: 125.
[9] I believe in God.

saintly father. Everything was the same for him. It did not make any difference whether he had a big bull or a slice of bread, gold, or soil.'

With that Lulu Khan turns to me and says:

'I have heard this story of Mekrus effendi many times in the past, Behram, but every time I hear it, the story becomes more powerful and meaningful. With every telling, I learn something new, and my soul becomes more enriched.'

He looks at his wife as if he wants to amplify the truth about her story. He then turns to me as if he wants to clarify the goodness about his father-in-law.

'As far as I know, the blessed Mekrus effendi was a generous man, and he had no interest in worldly goods. Although he was a wealthy man, he was not at all worldly-minded. I still do not know and no one knows why he never attempted to go on pilgrimage to Mecca. Only God knows. Maybe he worshipped and prayed within himself. It was as if God had freed him from religious duties because of his goodness and kind-natured heart. He was like that – kind, good-hearted, and generous. I remember when I was young like you. The year we got married – as a matter of fact, he died that year – yes, that year he said to me one day: "Lulu Khan, may all my sins rest on your shoulders if you don't tell me whenever you are in need of something." I am not sure if people like him have any sins. May God have mercy on him. He told me clearly, "Whatever you need, you must tell me."'

I see Lulu Khan glance at his wife with grateful eyes. I realise that everything they have was left to them by Lady Geshtina's father. Lulu Khan continues talking.

'I then told that kind-hearted man my wish. Since that day, Behram, we have not been in need of anything – God knows, even Lady Geshtina knows – don't you, Lady Geshtina?'

Lulu Khan doesn't wait for an answer. He turns to me as if I am a family member. I realise that he wants and expects me to believe his words, which I do. He then continues in his simple way.

'Who says that life is a test, life is a painful, life is a burden, and its duties are heavy? Not at all! Look, Lady Geshtina and I have travelled through the worldly life with its abundance, fruitfulness, and we have reached the border of death. But believe me, Behram, we have not the tiniest bit of worry or fear for death. God has created everything with a meaning. He has created every object with specific qualities, which has a meaning in itself for its surroundings and for everything else. Firstly, thanks to God and his divinity and also to my deceased saintly father-in-law, until today I have not known what it is like to be in need and poverty or in pain and distress. No, I really don't know what all that is in real life. Thanks to God, Lady Geshtina and I have worn and torn thirty-three pillows together. We are wealthy. We have always had love and compassion for each other, and we still do. We have two lovely, healthy children, one of each gender, as spices to our love. We have had it good until today. Jealousy, slander, and depravity are not familiar to us. We have lived virtuously and given alms. We have tried to fulfil our duties according the pillars of the faith at the right times and places.

'Haci Lady Geshtina and I headed towards the holy Mecca, and we circled the Kaaba there and touched the black stone with our foreheads seven times. Yes, we ran to and from between Al-Safa and Al-Marva seven times. We prayed and worshipped God one whole afternoon at Arafat. We stayed the night at the hill of Mirzaliye, a place near Mecca, between mount Arafat and the valley of Mina. In Mina we pelted Satan with stones and drove him away. In the Eyd el Qurban, we sacrificed an animal. May God not get displeased and annoyed with my words, but to cut the long story short, we have had a perfect life. I believe that we have lived the life the Lord has given to us according to his conditions and wishes.

'Anyhow, please forgive us, God, if we have got any ill-gotten gains or if anything sinful has been mixed in even as a single breath or a single heartbeat of ours… Please, God, be merciful to us for our sins!'

'Amen,' I say, and I think for myself: Who says that death does not allow you to fulfil yours duties or wishes? A faultless life full of righteousness and a strong faith – that is what I see on the faces and in the hearts of these good people.

With a belief and pride in being faithful and divine to God, Lulu Khan wants me and Lady Geshtina to go with him to the *kerge*[10], which is north of the vineyard. And so we do.

We all three stand up, leave the castle, and head north.

---

[10] Vineyard house, a small house containing all the equipment to press and boil grape juice to make sweets.

Up in the sky, the sun has done more than half of its daily journey and is heading west to set. We are leaving their courtyard and walking beside the vineyard, which runs parallel with the garden wall towards the north where the kerge is laid. The path we are walking on is narrow. The wind from the north is so soft that it gently massages my chest and heart. The waves of the wind are in such harmony that it is hard to describe in words. I have never ever had such a feeling before.

I don't know why, but I get such a strange and warm feeling. If I knew that God would not be annoyed or get offended in such a situation, I would ask the Lord to stop the time and freeze everything, as if it were a colourful wool mat of *kulav*[11], so that the soft wind would never stop blowing, so that this vineyard would never come to an end.

As I mentioned before, the path we are taking is small and narrow. Those paths are called vineyard paths in this region. The path makes us walk in a single file as if we were *peshmergas*[12].

---

[11] Wool that is soaked and beaten until the threads adhere very tight.

[12] Peshmerga is the term used by Kurds to refer to armed Kurdish freedom fighters, literally meaning 'those who confront death'.

Lulu Khan and his wife want me to go first, and they walk behind me, but I refuse to walk ahead because of my way of being brought up and say no, no way, and I walk after them. Whilst walking behind them in this narrow vineyard path, I turn around, and on the east side, I see autumn's flaming colours more clearly. I see how the soft, caressing wind blows away the vine leaves from the vine plants and the leaves of the pear trees from side to side. The yellow- and red-spotted pears are exposed and bunch of grapes are shining like glass when the leaves blow from side to side. The valleys and hills are now in shadow, and the mountain is waiting to be robed in shadow as the sun sets.

I realise that in autumn, especially around here in mid-autumn, everything seems to separate into balanced halves, creating a harmony of opposites, such as "to be or not to be", pain and happiness, life or death. Everything acts in harmony, like freshly baked hot bread and spring onions. That is exactly what has happened to me now, walking alone on this narrow vineyard path. Such a harmony has overtaken my heart and my overloaded brain.

I walk slowly behind Lulu Khan and his wife, in harmony with their steps, walking upward to the kerge. The more I walk, the more I like it, and I wish the journey would never end. I do not want the path to finish. I want to be able to walk as long as I want, and I want to think as much as I like. And I do so.

I no longer hear what my fellow travellers are saying. I think about the divine reason for the existence of all creation in detail and become absorbed in it: life, which has come and is passing by; all the things I have been thinking about in life; all the things I have been aware of and their meanings, things that are not easy to understand. I think about all those things and much more as I walk behind them, and finally I think about the story of Mekrus effendi. The more I think, the better I understand the deep meaning of that story. As I walk, the path seems to be getting narrower and longer. My soul is overwhelmed by an intensely emotional and indescribable feeling. Without knowing why, I feel deep down in my soul that I am going to cry. How can I explain it? I want to cry, but I don't know why. I feel that my eyelids are getting heavier, I feel sleepy but I continue walking.

While I am deep down in my soul and in my thoughts, the voice of Lulu Khan brings me up to the surface. He turns around, lifts his hand, and points at the mountain slope.

'Over there, Behram. There is the grave of Mekrus effendi, my father-in-law's grave, may God be merciful to him. May he rest in peace.'

I look up to where he is pointing. On the mountain slope where the vineyards end, between high, slippery cliffs near the mouth of some caves is what looks like the ruins of an antique city. On the east side of the caves there is a grave designed like a monument. The white dome that sticks out between the trees looks like the Jewish kippa. It is strange. I wonder why they have buried him there because the place is not a cemetery, nor does it look like a holy pilgrimage site. I do not ask. I assume that it is because his holy personality permeates the site, such as the one I just heard about.

Walking at the same speed as my fellow travellers, we reach the north side of the vineyard, on the mountain slope where the cliffs and caves are.

We head towards Mekrus effendi's grave first. It looks more like a monument than a grave, and its construction reminds me of igloos – white and round. The only difference is that igloos are made of ice, and this grave is made of white stone. The upper side of the monument is brown, which reminds me of a Jewish kippa. After lifting our hands up and praying for the soul of Mekrus effendi, Lady Geshtina turns to me and says:

'He constructed his grave himself, may God have mercy on his soul! He wanted a grave like this and instructed us as follows: "Place my dead corpse on the sekûk inside, put an earthenware jug of water by my head, and block the gate with a stone wall." We did as he told us after he died. We acted according to his wishes, and that is why he is on his own here.'

We leave the grave and look at the caves. One of them is very big, and the spring that feeds the lush vegetation originates from the bottom of the big cave. Lulu Khan tells me that the spring is named the Black Spring. When you enter the cave, you realise straight away that it has hosted a big ancient civilization. There are window like seats, sekûk, and shaped stone tables. All of them seem to be carved from one single piece of rock.

Lulu Khan says that they call it the big cave as it is the largest of all the caves around here. Who knows, people may have used this place as a guest room or as a meeting place. On the upper part of the cave, there is a stone sculpture of a fat, naked woman with big breasts, ornamented with raised design. The water from the roof of the cave is dripping down on the woman, down to her big breasts, and finally reaches the ground via her two nipples, drop by drop. The water has made a big hollow where all water collects on the ground. Lady Geshtina explains for me.

'The dried-up women and brides, the breastfeeding women and brides who have given birth and have not got milk in their breasts yet, still come here and drink the dripping water from the puddle. They hope and believe that they will then have milk in their breasts to feed their children.'

She then tells me the story of it. In the words of Lady Geshtina:

'According to legend, there was a family living here, a mother and two children – a grown-up daughter and a breastfed baby. One day their mum was working in the fields and was late coming home. The baby had got hungry and was crying and crying. He was so hungry and was crying so bitterly that made his sister heartbroken. She felt helpless and didn't know what to feed him with. She was so upset that she picked up her baby brother and came to this cave. She drank the water from the puddle under this stone woman and prayed that her breasts would fill up with milk. Her prayers were granted. A divine miracle happened to the virgin girl, and her breasts filled with milk. Legend has it that the girl had breastfed her brother until her mum returned home. It is said to be the divine work of these stones. That is a strong belief even today.'

◆

The ground in front of the caves is full of rocks. There are hollows, dug basins, cisterns, and the trace of water trenches. The biggest trench is still functioning. It flows from Black Spring. A little further down, on an open field like a harvest field, is a big pool that the water flows to, carved out from one of the big stones. The water fills up and flows over the pool, then runs to an open channel through a gutter and flows parallel to Lulu Khan's vineyard and downward.

The pool has steps and is round, which reminds me of the antic theatres. The steps widen from the bottom to the top and finish off like bracelets made of stone. On the upper north side of the pool there is a single big piece of a rock. It is as high as a tall man and has a shape of a cylinder. A seat has been carved inside the rock. There are seven holes all around the stone cylinder. Outside there are grooves carved like steps for climbing up to the seat. The steps are all worn down, which is a sign of how old they must be.

As soon as I see this cylinder-shaped rock with holes, the first impression I get is that it looks like an astronomical tower used for studying the sky and planets, and that astronomers must have sat here to observe the universe. However, according to Lulu Khan:

'This pool was a lake for jinns and fairies, and this big rock was a hiding place for the rulers of that time when out hunting. According to legend, the monarchs would come and sit here and watch the fairies come to the lake to wash them. It is said that many times … *many* times they used to attack their clothes with a packing needle to stop them from escaping!'

I believe this, for I believe in jinns and fairies, but I still think this big cylinder looks more like an astronomical observatory than a hiding place. Based on what Lulu Khan has told me, I get curious and ask him if any of the past rulers ever succeeded in catching a fairy. Lulu Khan answers yes to my question. According to myths, there has been such a person. However, the hunter was not one of the rulers but a shepherd. Again Lulu Khan says:

'Once upon a time, there was a shepherd working for an Emir. On one of God's days, he was pasturing his cattle around here. The bushes and trees were much denser in those days. The shepherd hung his food bag on the branch of the one of the trees near this pool, and then he sat in this cylindrical stone seat with seven holes. He was not aware of the purpose of this construction.

'After a while, he suddenly saw a girl under the tree on which he had hung his food bag. The girl took her dress off, put it under the tree, and went down to the pool to wash her hair. Her skin was as white as egg white and as clear as clear honey. Her dress matched her skin colour. It must have been God's providence, for suddenly a strong wind blew the shepherd's food bag from the tree, and it landed on the girl's dress. After the girl had washed her hair, she returned to the tree to get dressed. However, she couldn't touch her dress because the food bag on the top of her clothes had two metal chains. The girl stood back from her clothes and started crying. She cried a lot. The shepherd climbed out of the cylinder, looked shyly at the girl, and then looked down and asked the girl why she was crying. Whilst trying to hide her privates with her hands and with her long hair, she begged him to remove his food bag so she could get her dress. The shepherd didn't understand why she was behaving like that. He turned his head away and said: "Go and remove the food bag yourself. I won't watch you." The girl explained that she could not get to her dress because the food bag that fell on her clothes from the tree has two metal chains, and fairies cannot touch metal. Now the shepherd understood her behaviour. He said: "I will remove my food bag from your clothes on one condition only: if you marry me!" In her helpless situation, she could do nothing other than accept his condition. The shepherd removed his food bag with metal chains. The fairy gathered up her clothes and got dressed, and they headed towards his home.

'The shepherd lived with his old mother. They were poor. They named the fairy Perizade, which means "fairy-born, very beautiful". From the time Perizade entered their house, their home seemed to be blessed. Everything she touched or used became abundant. Whatever she cooked or baked filled up again after they had eaten. If she used a handful of salt, the same handful would be in the jar again. If she used a bowl of flour to bake bread, the same amount would be replaced. When she took a spoonful of butter for cooking, that exact spoonful would be in the dish. To cut the long story short, whatever she used up, the same amount replaced it.'

Next to the lake of fairies and jinns, where the cliffs end, there is kerge. We stop under a wild pear tree between the pool and the kerge, where the rocks meet up with red soil, and Lulu Khan tells us about the kerge.

Lulu Khan, Lady Geshtina, and I are sitting on a rug made of goat hair, placed on a sekûk, under the wild pear tree. They have built the sekûk under the tree. It is higher than the kerge and the pool. From here, I can see the pool, the basin, the place where the juice is – pressed out of the grapes, and the big cauldron where the grape juice is boiled to get a thicker consistency. If anyone asks me how the grapes are pressed for the juice, or how it is boiled, I can tell everything as if it's a tale like the one Lulu Khan just told me.

Lady Geshtina looks down the hill and cries, 'There are the children. Here come Nagina and Aryan.'

She says that they have been to the village to buy white sheets called *sawan* to spread the thick boiled grape juice on for drying to make a winter sweet called *bastêx*. That is how I find out that the boy is called Aryan.

Both of them drop the sheets on the edge of the pool and walk towards us. After greeting me with God's greeting, Aryan welcomes me. 'Oh! That is our guest!' he says and stretches his hand out to me. Then Nagina greets me by shaking my hand. They tell me that their father has told them about me.

'Yes,' I reply. 'I said yes to Lulu Khan's invitation, and here I am. It is a beautiful place here: watery, green, abundant, like God's heaven – a dream place. It is obvious that people from past time discovered this beautiful place and settled here to live.'

After a short conversation, including a few short questions and answers between me and Aryan, he turns to his parents and tells them that he has made sixty sawan for bastêx. Nagina stands up, picks up a small basket, and walks towards the vines. She fills her basket with grapes and pears. She then goes to the pool, dips the whole basketful of grapes and pears into the water to rinse them, and then comes back and places it in front of us to eat.

Lulu Khan tells me that they will start to boil the grape juice tomorrow, and he starts to explain the whole procedure. The special basin made for pressing the juice out is rinsed out first. The fireplace where the big cauldron is going to be placed is dug and set in the ground. The grapes are placed in a stone basin where the juice is pressed out. The juice that is pressed out of the grapes runs through a hole into another basin, which is lower than the first one. The sediment is then put in a big, thin cloth sack and taken to another workbench like a mangling device, called *îskince* to squeeze the rest of the juice out of it. The juice is then put in a big cauldron, placed on the fire, and boiled till it gets thick, like a pancake mixture. The mixture is then spread thin all over clean sawans and hangs on strings to dry. Walnuts or almond nuts are put on strings and get dipped into the boiled thick grape juice a few times, and then they get hung for drying. That is called *sincoq*.

He tells me a lot of other interesting things that I had not heard until now, but despite the novelty of this information, my attention is more on their children, Aryan and Nagina. They don't look like country people, nor are they as religious as their parents. How can I explain that impression I got? Their daughter Nagina is bareheaded. When she greeted me, she didn't lower her eyes like country girls do. She doesn't act like a pious person or like the daughter of a religious man by hiding herself from men who are strangers. She shook my hand like the daughter of an emir when she greeted me.

Also, both of them are so like each other. If the boy didn't have short hair and that newly grown hair on his overlip, and if the girl wasn't wearing a dress, one would not be able to say which of them is Nagina and which Aryan. It is the first time that I have seen twins being so alike. It is just … it must be due to female delicacy that Nagina is taller and thinner while Aryan is tubbier and has more of a strong young man's body. Otherwise, they are like a copy of each other: their mouths, their lips, their noses, their cheekbones, their eyes, their eyebrows … Their eye colour is yellowish like a lion. They are very sweet. You want to look at them all the time. I say 'look at them', and suddenly I wonder if the reason they moved up here was to keep the family away from everyone, from evil eyes. Thinking that they are sweet allows me to say to Geshtina with a smile, 'May God bless the youths! Wow! How like each other they look!'

I say 'youths'. It is not my nature to act big-headed, but their sweet looks and behaviour allow me to call them youths, which would suggest that I am much older than them, but in reality, they must be three years younger than me, maximum. Responding to my comments, Lady Geshtina turns to me with a smile like mine.

'Yes, they are! They don't just look like each other, they cannot live without each other. They are so bound to each other that they even feel each other's pain. If one of them has a headache, the other one feels that pain as well.'

Aryan and Nagina – two youths who feel each other's pain – look at each other and smile at the comment their mother just made. She points at a wooded area on the west side of us and continues.

'There … Once, on that slope, Aryan was cutting some wood, and Nagina was at home, kneading dough in the hall. Lulu Khan and I were sitting in the hall. Suddenly Nagina lifted her hand from the dough. She said: "I have pain in my thumb," and walked away. I sat by the big dough bowl and took over the kneading. By the time I had kneaded the dough and covered it, Nagina was still complaining about that pain in her thumb. She said she was worried that something had happened to Aryan. We headed quickly to the wooded slope. When we reached it, we saw Aryan sitting down with a bandage around his thumb. It was true. Aryan had cut his thumb with a pruning hook. I remember it was his left thumb.'

Aryan lifts up his left hand and shows his thumb with a smile. 'Yes, it was this thumb,' he says.

This incident, which Lady Geshtina just has told, sounds like a holy miraculous sign to me. Curious, I ask Aryan if he feels the same way about Nagina. Aryan looks affectionately at his sister and answers, 'I don't know. I have not felt it yet.' Then he adds, 'Maybe that's because she hasn't had any pain or been in trouble yet.'

We all laugh lightly at his last words, and Lady Geshtina starts mumbling some prayers quietly. 'May God spare everyone pain and trouble, and we as well, inshallah!'

'Amen,' I say, and I feel that they are a harmonious family. I feel very happy with this family and feel that I love this family very much. I can see how much they love each other and God. It is not up to me to comment on God's behalf, but I can feel how much God loves them as well. If you are religious, you remember that every incident, everything that happens, has a meaning, and it reminds you that it must be the divine wonders of God. Maybe that is why I recall the special characteristics of the prophet Job's family. I think for myself that maybe this family is the second family that God loves.

Although I have known this family for only a short time, seeing this place, their house, listening to the stories of these old couples, the respectful behaviour of their children, the family warmness – all this has made a big impact on me. I have to admit I have not met people and a family like this before. Although they practice the foundation teachings of Islam, they don't look like today's Muslims. They don't act like a family from our time. May God not get offended, but it seems to me that they don't belong to this world. Rather, they belong to heaven. It is as if there is a heavenly sign in this family's existence. They are happy, satisfied with their God, with their own existence, with their life – a life without pain and without grief, away from gossips and talking, purified from good and bad attributes. They live as they feel and they talk as they think. A perfect life and perfect people: That is what they believe and what they say, and that is how I also see it. I see that God has not only given

44

some humans part of his form. Our Lord has also given some of his unique elements to some people.

The friendly intercourse of this elderly couple and the harmony of the family strengthen my faith in God. Indeed, I feel that knowing this family has brought me closer to God. I understand better now that everything created by God has a meaning. Knowing that gives my soul a special calmness and strength. I feel that my doubts and hesitancy, which sometimes convinced my soul that the bad always wins in life, are disappearing. Now I see myself as in a different place and in a different time. I feel like one of the family members, and, as time goes by, I grow warm to them, to their words, to their behaviours, and to this place. All this makes me want to live longer.

Aryan tells his father that he wants to light the fire under the cauldron to check if the chimney is working properly. He then looks over his shoulder at Nagina and asks her to bring him a few buckets of water to pour into the cauldron.

Nagina throws a sweet glance at me, at her parents, and at her brother. 'OK,' she says and gets to work. After transporting several buckets of water from the pool to the cauldron, she starts washing the newly sewn sawans they brought from the village.

Aryan starts chopping wood for the fire. Lulu Khan, Lady Geshtina, and I are still sitting under the wild pear tree. I watch everything that is going on, all the things I am telling you right now. Yes … What was I was going to tell you now?

As I said, the special features, the unique elements, and the mysterious behaviours of the youths draw my attention in a sacred way. I realise that my attention, my smiling glances, and my facial expressions are noticed by the youths. I realize that Nagina especially is following me with her eyes. She sometimes looks at me over her shoulder as she does her chores. She watches me with ardour. I don't know why, but it gives me scary excitement every time she throws me one of those glances, and I don't dare look at her. When I say dare, it doesn't mean that I don't want to. I want it more than anything else and more than anyone else does. I am scared because I see how every glance from those eyes warms my soul, making my blood overheat. I realise that such attractive looks can change one's life, and, God knows, that is what I am scared of.

Those first darts from her eyes when she just looks at me again pierce my heart deeply, though I experience a sense of joy rather than heartache. Despite the long time, even today I still feel the joy of that moment, the happiness of that heartache. I don't know where that happy pain comes from. I still don't know whether it came from heaven in the sky or from hell beneath the earth. Only God knows.

It must be from one or the other. Wherever it comes from, the pain makes me face my weaknesses. I realise that I have other sides to my personality that I wasn't aware of till now.

The sense of comfort and feeling of freedom I had a moment ago seems to have flown away. For the first time in my life, I have to face a feeling of shame and recognise how forbidden glances can squeeze me to embarrassment and make me sweat inappropriately. My body feels hot and distressed, and I feel guilty that I cannot control my feelings. I say guilty because I see myself pulling the sin towards myself. I feel sinful looks and sinful thoughts spreading all over my body and personality like a malignant disease.

But there is one thing I don't get. I cannot understand why my faith, my piety, and my belief in God, does not put a stop to this and prevent me from committing sins. I cannot understand why my faith and belief don't push me away from all those sinful crimes. I feel like a scorpion trapped inside a circle of fire and watching this danger, this illness, and this sin. I see how God is turning his back to me. He is leaving me alone and walking away.

I feel so lonely with this state of mind. The sun is very close to setting, but it hasn't disappeared yet. It is as if even the sun is keeping its golden and reddish light for a holy purpose.

Aryan is placing the wood he has cut under the cauldron. Nagina is washing the sawans, squeezing the water out of them, and placing them on one side. She has a chiffon dress on. She has folded the skirt of her dress up and secured it under her belt, and she has rolled her trousers up above her knees. She dips the sawans, one by one, in the water, places them on the big stone platform beside the pool, and tramples on them with her bare feet. It seems to me that she is not stamping on the sawans with her sacred feet, but rather is doing a celestial dance, as if she wants to show me what she can do, as if she is rebelling, as if she is committing a sin and making me the culprit.

Until today, I had not witnessed how the grapes are harvested, the juice is pressed out, and the grape juice is boiled. I had not closely observed the work and daily chores of country people, and, until now, the appealing and miraculous ways of women and girls had not come to my attention. I am sunk in thought, and I put my present uncomfortable feelings down to my first real experience of the country lifestyle. I think that I see now why country people fall in love at an early age and marry young. But I am also aware that talking to myself in this way doesn't draw my attention and feelings away from Nagina, from her lips, her body wrapped in that chiffon dress, her white legs like white cheese, her eyes like fire, her corrupting looks, her beauty, and her virginity.

Every time she stamps on the sawan, the water squirts between her toes high up to her calves and then runs down from her calves again. The water drops from her legs are shining in the sunlight. I try hard, but I cannot manage to stop watching her – an unpleasant and sinful situation, a time and place for guilty feelings and thoughts.

Not to get away from sinful thoughts, but to prevent Lulu Khan and Lady Geshtina from realising that I am interested in their daughter, I ask their permission to walk to the caves. I tell them I am going to look at the works of art inside the caves. As you also already realise and know, I am lying. Yes, that is what I do. I stand up and walk away from Lulu Khan and Lady Geshtina and walk towards the caves.

I feel that their daughter has seduced me and will drive me to sinful actions. On the way I think about her, I see her in the caves, only her. There is only her and no one else. I don't see anything else, neither those ancient works of arts of patterns and embroideries around the entrances of the caves, nor those embossed pictures that are embedded in dampness and darkness. My fixation on Nagina has built a wall of bricks before my eyes, preventing me from seeing anything else but her. I don't see anything else. Everything except her is dark. Nothing in the world can take my thoughts away from her and protect me from sinful feelings. I am sure that I am in love. I realise, like all people who are in love, that love is like a weed that grows anywhere and anytime. No one knows when and where it will grow. A saying comes to my mind – I don't remember where I heard it: "Love is a beautiful scent that spreads quickly and which one can smell instantly". I am worried about the smell permeating everything. I am worried that my love will also spread all around and about and reach Nagina's parents. I am scared that they will have an inkling of it.

In this state of mind, I leave the caves and head towards the vineyard house and the pool. I stop at the big cylindrical rock by the pool – the one that looks like an astronomical observation tower and is supposed to have been a hiding place for hunting monarchs. The reason I stop by this rock is not that I am interested in history or archaeology. No, I know myself. It is not because of that. My purpose is devilish, because from here I can see Nagina more clearly. I walk around the rock to the steps and climb up inside the rock in order to be able to see Nagina better. I understand now why Lulu Khan calls this a hideout. When sitting inside, no one can see you from the outside, but you can see everyone and everything around you easily and clearly through the seven holes. I can see the sky, the mountain, and the far away houses in the village, the vineyards, the kerge, the pool, and Nagina from here. I see her better from here than from under the wild pear tree. I watch her better from this stone shield without anyone knowing about it.

No one except God knows that I watch Nagina, sitting in this ancient astronomical observing tower. Not Lulu Khan, not Lady Geshtina, not Aryan – no one. I don't want them to know. In other words, I hide the vulgar and sinful sides of my personality. I want them to believe that this place – in their words the hunting shield, the pool, the lake of jinns – has caught my interest and attention, and that is why I am sitting here. But you and God know that it is not true and not the real reason. Oh please, God, save me from my sinful behaviour!

Yes, as I said, I am sitting in the stone hideout from where I can master everything and see everything well. The water is still squirting between her toes and up over her knees and dripping down to her calves. She is still dipping the sawans one by one in the pool, stamping on them with her feet, lifting them up to squeeze the water out, and putting them aside to hang up later for drying. Her dress is still shining in the sun. She is facing the other way now, and I can see only her back.

I don't know whether she knows that I am in sitting in here, but I can see her from here. I can see how she squeezes the water out of the last sawan and puts it on top of the others, how she takes off her chiffon dress and puts it aside. Why is she doing that? Now she is left with a transparent white silk underdress that allows me to see all her body features. As I said, her back was towards me. She looks like a peeled white poplar tree.

Lulu Khan and Lady Geshtina are sitting by the fire. Aryan brings some more wood and puts it on the fire under the cauldron. Sitting here inside this den makes it possible to see everything. I see them, but I don't want them to see what I see. I don't want them to see their own daughter with a transparent underdress. I don't want them to know that I have seen their daughter like that. I know if I leave my confinement I will be embarrassed, Nagina will be offended, Lulu Khan and Lady Geshtina will be ashamed of the situation, and God knows what Aryan will think.

So as not to cause any of the above to happen, I stay where I am and imprison myself there like the hunted rather than the hunter, like a fly trapped in a bowl of honey that cannot get out. I bow my head and talk to myself. Maybe she just wants to wash her face and neck after working and sweating all day along. That is what I think and expect. I sit in the stone den with my head bowed, waiting for Nagina to wash herself and put her dress on so I can get out. My head is bowed and my eyes closed. I don't know how long I sit in that position.

When I lift up my head and look around me, I see that the light and colours that were there have completely disappeared. There is no sun. A thick, dark layer of red ochre has covered the surface of the whole world. It is as if the sun is shining on the earth through a thick, dark red cloth; as if there is dust raining from the sky; as if a shadow is raining from the sky; as if darkness is raining down from the sky. Such a colour has dressed the sky and the earth that no poet could describe it. It is so strange, neither day nor night. I look all around towards the caves, the vineyard, and the trees surrounding the vineyard. Everything is the same colour, like a sepia-coloured picture. Everything is washed out. It is like the earth has caught fire and everything is static in this state.

And just at that moment, as if someone were calling me from the pool, as if a magical power were calling me towards itself, I strive to get out of the stone den. Hesitantly, I try to go towards the magical voice and pool. It is a huge balk. God knows, I have never, ever stumbled or doubted like this before. Why this hesitation now? I don't know. I cannot see Lulu Khan. Lady Geshtina is not there and neither are Aryan or Nagina. Nagina is not where she was before. I must be confused. I don't know where I am. Everything I have seen and have told you up to now feels like a big lie. I don't believe that I have seen or experienced any of it.

Although I am aware that I should not be doing it, I stand up in the stone den so I can see well. I look carefully at the pool. I can see better now. Please, God! Don't make me a sinner! Nagina has taken her white, transparent, silky underdress off and put it on the top of her outer dress, and she is lying on her back in the water, totally naked. Her face is turned towards the sky, towards God. She is facing the sky and God.

Time after time, she throws her head back and dips in the water, fills her mouth with water, lifts her head up, and bends forward, squirting the water on her chest. I don't know why she is doing this. Every time she squirts, a mouthful of water pours down her chest. The water is running between her perky breasts, down to her belly button, and continues to flow downward after swirling around her belly button.

Down from her belly button – down there ... Please, God! Please save me from being a sinner! Her privates are not visible to me from here, but I can see a bunch of hair where her intimate part is that is the same colour as her head hair. I can see how the water runs down her pubic hair and disappears. Every time she bends her head backward and dips into the water to fill her mouth, it is only then that our eyes meet. And every time ... I am ashamed and disgraced before you, my God! Every time I cannot turn my eyes away from her, I cannot stop myself watching her. I do not cover my eyes with my hands and turn my head away. I don't know why. The sin is so attractive, and it is dragging me so hard that I want this situation to last forever. Neither do I ask help from the holy verses and try to take refuge in those words, nor do I ask pardon of God. I swear, if it was somewhere else, in another time, or if I was facing a different sin, I swear I would open my hands towards the sky, I would bow down on my knees on the threshold of the church or mosque and pray to be forgiven for the sins I have committed, and I would weep inwardly. But for the first time I want to prolong this sinful experience, this sexual desire.

I don't want just to watch. I want to lean on her and hunt for her as well. The words of Lulu Khan's description of the stone den are correct: It is a hunting place, a place for hunting fairies. A voice inside my head says that the fairy is Nagina and no one else. I get confused. My heart is of two minds, and however much I try, I cannot find a way out. But Nagina finds her way out. She seems to be happy about her swimming and washing. Cheerfully she walks towards the stone den, towards me, without bothering to cover her privates with her hands or hair. At that moment I feel that there is only her and me on this planet, just me and her in this time, in this world.

My sinful feelings are defeating me. It is as if they are becoming my new religion. It is as if a new faith, a new disease and desire, has taken over my soul. God is so far away that I cannot reach him with my hands, so far away that I cannot make myself be heard, so far away that I cannot see him with my eyes. God has left me all alone here. He has abandoned me. There is only one thing. The only thing I see in front of my eyes at that moment is her: Nagina and her mystical naked body. When I see her bare body, I realise how much of her beauty has been hidden under her clothes. Nakedness suits her better. Nagina is transformed into a houri. If she had a pair of transparent wings, I would think she was a fairy that had flown down from heaven and landed here.

It is said that the duration of desire for a naked woman is short and does not last long. I watch her for a short time but intensely. I see things in her that I have not seen or thought about before: a female and fecund body, a body with harmony from top to toe like on an Abyssinian's concubine, with the colour of an acorn of the valonia oak in the autumn season.

I see two firm and upright breasts with nipples like dark tattoos. Around her nipples, a button-sized embossment. Her wet, purplish, curly hair is hanging down to the nipples. The water dripping down from her hair and lovelocks looks like purple beads. Beneath her breasts is a sweet belly button, a belly button so sweet that makes me think of fermented dough with a finger print like a button and baked in a tandoor.

And the intensity of my gaze … May God forgive my sins! My eyes are focused on that belly button. I have never ever focused on something with that degree of intensity before. I have never ever felt such a strong desire. I have never seen a naked woman before. I have read simple, stupid poems describing the beauty of women: their tallness, their eye colour, how much they can be enjoyed … but no matter what others say, I think the sweetest, most sacred part of a woman's body must be her belly button, don't you think?

As I said, Nagina gets out of the pool totally naked and wet and starts walking towards me to the stone den. I get out of my hiding place and climb down. Outside, by the stone den, she stretches out her arms and encircles my shoulders. I am not sure, but that is what I feel. Like a newborn bird that has just discovered its wings, I lift my arms and put them around her neck. The heat and scent of her body and the smell of her nipples ravish me. I want to go further. I want to stretch my hands between her thighs. That secret thing is visible to me, that thing that the world rotates around it axis for. Yes, that is what catches my eye, and I see it. It is speckled. I watch it carefully, curiously. The speckling patterns that cover the two lips of her privates give a special colour and beauty to it. I feel that I am doing something without permission and start feeling afraid. At that moment, a voice fills my sinful ears. The voice gets louder: "Have you watched it properly, Behram?"

My God! Oh my God! Hearing my own name at that moment brings my flighty mind back. I become aware of my own existence again. I realise that I am Behram, Behram from Kawash, a student of the School of Theology. I have come to the village of my landlord, and I am in his vineyard, the vineyard of Lulu Khan from Argon. I don't see where the voice is coming from. I don't recognize the voice. I cannot differentiate whether the voice belongs to a man or a woman. After a few seconds, roughly three heartbeats, I lift my head with shame towards the voice, and, without my seeing him/her, the owner of the voice talks again.

"Yes, Behram, you didn't say anything. What did you understand from looking at those private places?"

This time I recognize the voice. It is Lulu Khan's. What shall I say? How can I face him? How can I tell him? Yes, I watched her carefully. And how will I be able to tell him where I particularly looked, what I understood, and how

I enjoyed it? How can I say all that? No, I can't! My head drops to my chest. I cannot get a sound out from the fear of embarrassment. Until you are embarrassed, you are not aware of the unacceptability of your actions. Some things are unknown to you until you experience them for yourself. You must live it and feel it directly. That is what I am going through and feeling right now.

The effect of hearing Lulu Khan's voice makes me feel ashamed, as if I am the naked one, not Nagina. My whole body feels tense from embarrassment. I start sweating, and I feel the sweat pouring out of every hair and every pore on my body ... and my eyes! Oh, my God! You may not believe this, but because of this distasteful situation, my eyeballs seem to have popped out of their sockets and are standing in front of me.

I no longer lift my head or make a sound. I don't answer Lulu Khan and don't want to see him. Shame and sins pour in on me. My head bows, and I stare down toward the ground at my feet. I don't know what to do, how to act. I want the ground to swallow me up, but it doesn't. I want to become a drop of water and sink into the arid soil and disappear, but no, it doesn't happen. Sometimes things do not happen, as you would like. When I realise that my wishes will not come true, I suddenly make up my mind.

Because of my sinful actions, I am angrier with God than with myself. I rebel against him for letting me live, for letting me commit more sins and feel more ashamed. God knows that is why, I now promise myself from now on to swear in my own name and not in the name of God and to do anything I want. I will do my own thing. As in the traditional act of repentance when one prostrates oneself or circumambulates the Kaaba during the pilgrimage in Mecca, I bend down and stroke my hand over the earth. I don't know what comes to my hand, but whatever it is, I hit my forehead with it with all the strength I have. I want to kill myself. My eyes are closed. At first everything is dark, and then a scarlet-coloured light makes circles in front of my closed eyes. I sit down because I can't stand up anymore, and I fall to the ground. My forehead touches the barren soil and is supported by the ground. It is the first time since the fight between Cain and Abel that I can smell the scent of blood on barren soil. I can feel the heat and smell from blood-soaked soil in my forehead, and I realise that I am thirsty.

I see that Nagina is still at the same place, in the same position, and still naked. Her body, her beauty, her scent, and her voice are getting closer. I can feel her, and I can hear her. I want to ask her if she would give me some water. Without me saying it, she understands my thirst. She hurries closer and looms over me. She widens her eyes and grabs her right breast, which makes me think that she wants to give me water from her breast.

I am aware ... I know very well that all these thoughts are sinful. Even now, telling you all this, I know even telling this story is a kind of sin, but ...

But Nagina turns away from me and walks to her clothes, picks up her white, silky, transparent underdress, throws it over her shoulder like an Indian woman, and walks in front of me half naked. Yes, she walks in front of me, and I walk behind her.

Nagina is in front of me, and we are walking. She is leading me. We are going to a spring. She doesn't tell me that, but I know it. There is a weris length distance between us. With her body, her full womanhood, her scent like a path, and hope, she is in front of me, and I am behind her. We are walking in hope of reaching water.

The road grows longer as we trek through meadows and valleys. I don't know how many days journey we have done. I get the feeling that since the day I started to walk I have been on the go without stopping and that till the end of my life I will always be on the road, walking in search of hope.

I walk behind Nagina. I don't know what we are searching for. I have forgotten my thirst, and don't know why we are walking. My thirst has ceased, but my mouth, my lips, and my tongue are very dry. My tongue is so dry that I am not able to get it around a word to ask questions, to ask where we are heading. God knows I interpret my silence as being due to dryness in my mouth, and I think that is why I can't ask any questions. I am quiet, and she is quiet. I am behind, and she is in front of me.

We walk. It is late afternoon. We come across a very high mountain. It looks high and enchanted. It seems to be leaning against the stomach of the sky. It looks like a pillar holding up the sky. It is very close to God, closer than mounts Hira and Sinai. The top of the mountain is still covered with snow from long ago. From this distance, from down where we are, it looks as if someone has poured an earthenware jug filled with yoghurt on the top of it. The white snow is still shining reddish under the sun. I say still because the last beams of the sun are only on the top of the mountain. I realise that the sun is always going down later on the top than down here. Light and dark patches of clouds gather and form a belt around the waist of the mountain. God knows that no other clouds will reach the top of the mountain, except for snow clouds. Not only God knows, even I know that! The clouds are spreading down to the deep valleys now.

The path on the slope is not a common path for other travellers or caravans. It is as if it was made only for us, as if we are making this path for ourselves as we walk, as if we are making the way of our destiny and then walking along it. The road is empty.

Some way up the slope, there is a jet of water spurting from the rocks. It looks as if someone had put a knife in the stomach of the mountain and the water is gushing from it. The water hits the rocks around. It froths up and runs downward. Nagina and I are standing down on the slope by the running water from the spring. We wash our hands and faces and drink some water. We lie on the ground by the water next to each other and rest. The night and the silence have taken over everything and everywhere.

The darkness hugs us and wraps around us so that we disappear into the night. The sound of the running water seems to be singing only for us, for our silence. I say silence because Nagina and I are still quiet and not talking as if silence has become a language between the two of us and we have learned that language and that is why we are quiet. There is no word, good or bad, wise or foul coming out of our mouths. My eyelids feel heavy in this silence and loneliness, and after a while they start closing and staying closed. I don't know for how long they stay like that.

The first thing I see when I open my eyes is the moon. It looks like a big, white, round tortilla. All above us, from the top of the mountain down to the feet of God, is clear and bright. Only snow clouds can make it to the top of the mountain. The slope of the mountain, where we are now, is covered with light and dark patches of clouds, and we find ourselves inside these clouds. I have never been so close to clouds in my life. Sometimes the clouds partly block the moon. It makes it look like a ship. It turns into a sky ship and fights against the cloud waves. The scene calls for the soul of a poet. Only a truly good poet would be able to describe the panorama, not me.

I sit up. I look and see that Nagina looks like a fairy in the water under moonlight. When she rises from the water and walks towards me, she looks like a shining silver statue, a water statue shining under the moonlight. I am now certain that Nagina and I are on our own here in this lonely and uninhabited mountain under the moonlight.

Being alone and on our own makes me aware of something. My brain, my heart, my feelings are telling me to do the same thing – to do what I want. In other words, the feelings I have at this moment, my thoughts … how can I say? I cannot explain how much I want her and how much I long for her and her body at this moment. Only God knows. My heart is boiling and beating so fast that it feels as if it is going to fly off, out through my ribs from inside my chest. This journey may be the first time I have truly expressed myself. I mean, I will – without feeling shy or ashamed – open my heart to a girl. Maybe that is why my heart is beating so intensely and loudly that I can hear nothing else.

'I want to tell you something, Nagina. No one knows. Only God and I know about it, and God and I want you to know it as well: I want you.'

The last three words come out of my mouth so quickly, that I am not sure whether they came out of my mouth or my heart. God only knows where it came from. But there is no sound coming from Nagina. She doesn't reply.

With calm steps, she walks towards me in her usual way. Like a sleepwalker, she walks slowly and quietly towards me. We are close to each other now. There is warm steam coming out from her wet lock of hair, from her wet chest and breasts, and her wet mouth and lips. It smells like hot milk. She bends over me with her wet body. Her lovelocks are covering my face, blocking out the moonlight, and the moon sinks into darkness. Those dark patches of clouds surround us on this mountain slope and suddenly turn to lightning and thunder. The sky becomes angry and pours rainwater on us.

This night the water is pouring on us, the water is pouring from us, water is pouring from the fissures in the rock, water is pouring from the spring and running away. It is a night like the ones described in tales. If I was sure that God would not be offended and become angry, I would say:

That night, only that night, at the slope of the mountain, was equivalent to all God's other days, equivalent to all the days donated to my life by God, on this earth.

But that dark, wet, and beautiful night alights on us suddenly. As soon as that holy night lightens, I realise how dreadful we look. We have got filthy and soiled by the wetness of the night. And it is not only us or the soil, where we have been lying and committing sinful actions. I see even the sky has become filthy. Yes, even the sky has become soiled and filthy with our sins. Those condensed white patches of cloud in the beginning of the evening have now become dark like tarmac around the mountain: black and dirty.

We are still covered in the night's filth. The reddish soil of the night has stuck to Nagina's legs and dried between her thighs. The colour of the soil looks like the colour of Holy Jesus' palm. We get rid of the holy dirt. We descend the mountain and come to lowland meadows and walk. Truly, she is walking in front of me and I am following her as usual. We communicate with each other without sound or talking, as if we are learning a new language. I start to learn her silence and quietness. I get used to her not talking and accept it.

Silence is also a language on its own, it does not even have verbs and pronouns. Silence is a superior and strong language with its meaning, wishes, and demands. I know that now. I say superior and strong language, because there are things, which you cannot describe or explain in words.

With our own special language, everything I come across, walking over mountains and through valleys, becomes unfamiliar and precious. Not even in my dreams have I seen these places. I don't know where we are. I don't know where and when, but there is a moment when Nagina slows down without stopping. Without turning towards me or talking to me, she lifts her hand and points to a hill further on. That is all. A hill made of soft, fine, and reddish soil. It looks like a hill of fire. We set out towards the hill.

When we get closer to the hill, I see that there is a single Crataegus tree on the crest. The tree is small, but its shadow is big enough for the three flocks of sheep to rest under. Nagina walks to the shadow of the Crataegus tree, bends her knee, and sits down as if she is praying. She then watches towards the north with a straight back and with gazing eyes. She is very quiet and still as if she is meditating. I don't know why, but I walk to her, I lie down, put my head on her knees, and close my eyes. The warmness and softness from her thighs reminds me of a familiar smell, like the smell of Siyabend felt by Xecé.[13] I understand now why one is happy to die in a situation like this. But funnily enough, I don't die.

When I wake up and open my eyes, I find myself under the Crataegus tree. My head is on the ground, but I cannot see Nagina. She is nowhere. It is the first time during the whole journey that she has left me alone and disappeared. I look around me. There is nothing: no mountain, no brushwood, no stones or rocks, no path or road. I am all by myself under the Crataegus tree on the top of the hill, lonely as God. I am far away from the feeling of fear. I feel no fear from loneliness, no fear from hunger or thirst. I am

---

[13] Siyabend û Xecé: A well-known love epic between a man and woman who are in love with each other. It is a famous tragic love story known by all Kurds, like Romeo and Juliet. Many songs, stories, and plays have been inspired from the story.

just curious and feel anxiety about Nagina's disappearance. I sit down and lean my back on the trunk of the tree. I think Nagina is playing a practical joke – like jokes one comes across many times during life.

With these anxious thoughts, I look down the hill. I see something that looks like a mirage coming towards the Crataegus tree – towards me. At first, I cannot make out what it is, but when it comes closer, I can see that it is a human being. It is difficult to see the face clearly from the mirage, but I am sure it is a man. He does not look like a traveller or a hunter, nor does he look like a peddler. When he is a few meters away, I stand up and try to walk towards him. I want to greet him with God's greetings and ask him who he is and where we are. But he stands still where he is, and I can't walk towards him, either. My legs will not carry me as if I have rheumatism in my knees and I cannot walk – as if there is a hidden power stopping me from getting close to him. I feel like a piece of chewing gum stuck to the ground under the tree and cannot move.

Without saying hello, he launches straight into a question.

'What good wind blew you here, my good man?'

'May God not deprive us of goodness! I don't know where this place is. A young girl named Nagina and I came here together.'

'Yes,' he says. 'You have named her Nagina and call her with that name, but her real name is Demora.'

In this barren land, I get interested in what this man says. However, I really don't understand what he means, and I don't argue with him. I don't ask him who he is, how he knows Nagina, and why Nagina's real name is Demora. At this moment, there is nothing more important to me than Nagina and her name. That is all that is on my mind.

Maybe that is why I ask him, 'Where has Nagina gone?'

'She went back home,' he says.

I suspect that he has something to do with Nagina coming and going. That is why I ask him reproachfully: 'How do you mean gone home? How could she go without me? She and I travelled together from far away. I still don't know where that place is.'

'That place is a place for good people', he says. 'Only good people can manage to reach there.'

'Will you do me a favour please? Tell me how can I find Nagina, or as you call her, Demora. We came here together. I want us to get back together. I want to go home, and I want to go to her.'

'I know,' he says. 'I know that is what you want. I know that is what has brought you here. But you are not blessed. You are not one of the *ehl-î-malê*[14].'

I don't let him see this, but I am hurt by his words. Besides hurting me, his words make me suspicious that he is aware of our journey. I still don't know who this man is, what kind of person he is. He is as strange as his words like 'not one of the ehl-î-malê'. I talk to him with curiosity and anxiety at same time.

'Please forgive my inexperience,' I say anxiously, 'but I didn't recognise you Mr ...'

'I am Mekrus,' he replies. 'I am Mekrus effendi, father of Lady Geshtina and grandfather of Demora.'

On hearing the name of Mekrus effendi, I feel warmth, a recognition, and closeness in my whole body.

---

[14] Domesticated.

'They have told me about you. They have told me about your goodness and kindness. I am not one of your family members, but I want you to do me a favour. I want you to treat me as one of your family and guide me. I want to find Demora and go back.'

'Go back where?'

With that question I feel as if my whole body has been blown by the wind and been made numb, and I cannot answer his question. I am not able to get my tongue around a single word. I don't know how to answer his question. I wait in silence, but he adds another question to his already-asked question.

'You don't answer? What do you say?'

He is still awaiting an answer. He wants to know where I want to go. I sit down. I take my shoes off to give me time to collect myself, and then I start to talk in a complaining and moaning manner in order to make him believe me.

'I don't know what to say and how to say it, Mr ... I feel ashamed before you and God. Nagina and I had such a long journey together that I have blisters on the soles of my feet. I don't know how much time has passed since our journey, but I really got used to her existence and her smell. I really love her. Believe me, Mekrus effendi ... believe me, I loved her more than I loved God.

'I believe you,' he says and looks me straight in the eye.

I don't know what he is thinking at that moment. If it were another time and another place, I would without doubt be scared and ashamed of his looks. But at this moment, I don't feel any fear or shame though his looks make me think about myself and my words. I become especially aware of my last sinful sentence. But I don't know now, nor did I know then, how those words got out of my mouth. Sinful words! To correct my sinful words or to give another meaning to my sin, I turn to Mekrus effendi and say: 'I want to contact Nagina, Mekrus effendi. I want to be with her and go back with her.'

Mekrus effendi looks down at the red soil as if he is going to reveal a secret. He repeats my words and continues in a scholarly manner.

'You want to contact Demora, you want to go back. But don't forget there are two things that the sons and daughters of Adam have not been able to do throughout their lives. The first thing is they will never be able to return to where they came from. The second thing is they will never be able to reach where they want to go. These are the two things that human beings cannot succeed in.'

He turns his face towards the north after speaking as if he now sees Nagina somewhere out there.

'She is not coming back. Demora came to take her time and fate on earth into her own hands, the fate that has been shaped by God's left hand. And that is one of the special features of the blessed ones, the domesticated ones, and is a holy gift.'

'This ehl-î-malê you talk of: Please, Mekrus effendi, forgive my inexperience. I have heard *ehlî-heq* and *ehlî-kitêb*[15], but not of the "domesticated ones." As I said, please be patient with my inexperience and my lack of knowledge, but I want to know and to learn about it.'

'The domesticated ones,' he explains, 'are particularly rebellious people. They are unbreakable and unbendable. They are *ehlî-dil*: good-hearted, good-natured people who

---

[15] Man of God and people of the book, i.e. Muslims and Christians.

listen to their hearts, wishes, and desires. What was it you wanted to learn?'

'Everything. I want to learn everything, Mekrus effendi – everything that I don't know.'

'Knowledge,' he murmurs thoughtfully, then after a moment's silence, 'You know that knowledge is a sin,' he says.

It is clear to me that whatever I do, whatever I say, he seems to find some way of objecting or disagreeing. When I mention Nagina, he talks about the domesticated ones. When I mention knowledge, he throws the word *sin* at me.

This makes me feel a little suspicious, and I say rather disgruntledly: 'I don't understand why knowledge is sinful. Didn't our prophet say: "The ink from a wise man's pen is more holy than the blood from a martyr"?'

'Don't believe it', he says. 'Let us not talk about the prophets now because no one listens to them anymore. They are no good to anyone anymore.'

'Thousands … I mean thousands and thousands of people are queuing in front of churches and mosques,' I argue. 'They wear out their elbows with studying at *madrasas*[16] in order to learn more and to find out about the truth.

Mekrus effendi gives me the following advice.

'Don't you believe those thousands and thousands! Don't forget: When the majority of people are heading somewhere and gathering together, the truth is not there, it is somewhere else. That is why you need to go from there and look for it somewhere else. The truth I am talking about, the knowledge and sin I mentioned, have always been the same. That is the deal. It has been like that from the time of the Great Emir, from the time of God.'

---

[16] Muslim theological schools.

Demora, one of the ehl-î-malê, the Great Emir, God and his commands, knowledge, and the sin of knowing: All these words of Mekrus effendi make me wonder whether he has communication with hidden powers. I don't want to tell him that, but I look at him in disbelief and curiosity. Simultaneously, I note that the mole on his face on the left side appears very beautiful and mystical to me.

He seems to notice my doubt. 'Don't worry,' he says. 'Don't be scared about bad things. The lord I am talking about has many names. His lords also have as many names and aspects as God. All those names have been selected by the sons and daughters of Adam, from the archangel to Satan.'

I feel a cold shiver run down my whole body when I hear the name Satan, and I want to curse him as always. I want to get rid of him – from me and everyone – with prayers and holy verses. I don't know why, but I cannot manage that, and God knows it is the first time I do not say 'damn the Devil'. As if a cursed wind has blown through my soul and thoughts, wiped away my feelings and made me numb, I realise that the only thing I want is to know more – to gain knowledge about many things, secret things, magical things, things that are believable or unbelievable. I am sure that I am going to learn many things from Mekrus effendi, things that have hidden meanings and are covered up.

Without thinking too much about what he said, I cry hastily: 'I want, Mekrus effendi, I still want to know. Even if knowledge is a sin, I want to know. I want to see the sins, I want to live the sins. I want to meet the big Lord, I want to go to Nagina …'

I realise quickly that I have made a mess of everything. Those are not my words. It is as if someone or something else – a hidden power – is making me say those things. The words just slip out of my mouth. I don't feel ashamed or scared of my words, but I feel uncertain as to whether they are good or bad. So I hang my head and ponder on what I have said and done.

Mekrus effendi seems to feel my uncertainty. He moves closer.

'Look into my eyes without feeling uncertainty, shame, or fear.'

I cannot avoid his eyes. I silently look into his eyes without any sense of uncertainty, shame, or fear. He comes closer, puts his hand on my forehead and starts mumbling something. I can't make out what language it is, but I think it is one of those mixed languages, one of the languages that God created at the tower of Babel and spread over the world. At that moment I realise that his act is a kind of sanctification ceremony, but Mekrus effendi doesn't give it a name.

'Now just follow me,' he says.

I realise that my feet are not heavy any more. My feet are light, my soul is light, my spirit and consciousness are light. I mean I have no doubts, no fear, and no suspicions any more. As if I am in a holy land and walking on a holy road, I leave my shoes – what is left of them after the journey – under the Crataegus tree and follow him with bare feet.

This time, Mekrus effendi and I are travelling together. I understand from the wind that we are heading towards the north. Suddenly, the wind becomes stronger and turns into a whirlwind that engulfs us, circles around us a few times, and stretches up to the sky like a pillar. It seems to be teasing and fighting us.

I pray for God's mercy and blessing in silence, but I still don't know whether my arrival, my journey, and my experience so far are auspicious. To ensure that we are going to Nagina, I ask Mekrus effendi where we are going.

'We are heading towards the place in your heart,' he replies.

I listen to my heart. I realise that Mekrus effendi not only is aware of our journey – my journey with Nagina – he also knows what is in my heart. And that is why I turn to him without feeling shy and say what is in my heart.

'Forgive my weakness, Mekrus effendi. I want Your Excellence to tell me something, to give me some advice.'

'*Kerem bike*[17], he says and points along the road we are walking on and continues. 'It is a sin to kill your wishes and desires. Since the creation of human beings, the most holy thing is man's desires. For the sake of peace of mind, a sound mind, and a strong, clean heart, one must listen to one's own wishes and act accordingly.'

And we walk on.

I think about my holy desires as I keep walking behind Mekrus effendi. I am not sure how long we have been walking or what we have been talking about during the journey. All I know since my meeting with Mekrus effendi is that my belief has changed, my thinking has matured more. In this new state of maturity, in Mekrus effendi's words, being one of the ehl-î-malê, I walk next to him now.

I realise that time has passed, and I find myself in a different time. It is me and him, in a different place, in a different time, and on a different road – a road leading to a tower. That is what it looks like from a distance. Mekrus

---

[17] Let's us go.

effendi lets me know that it is the Castle of Silence. We reach a meadow close to the Castle of Silence. Looking at its high walls and towers, I conclude it seems to be very old.

When we reach our destination, a young man with long hair and a black beard, wearing a kaftan like *yezîdchilgîr*[18] is there to meet us. He has a walking stick made of the terebinth tree in his hand. His eyes are yellowish like tiger eyes. He stands roughly seven steps away from us.

'Why are you so late?' he asks.

I don't know him. I keep quiet. To be honest, I expect Mekrus effendi to answer. Anyway, I don't know what to answer because I don't understand why he asks such a question. I don't know why we are late, and that is why I am quiet.

We go inside in silence. There she is, inside the hall, lying on a broad black stone. She is covered in white tulle, looking so innocent. I don't remove the tulle, but all her features – the broadness of her forehead, the shape of her lips and nose, her perky breasts and raised nipples, her belly button, the triangle part between her thighs – all those features of her firm and chaste body look like a statue made of transparent silk.

At that moment, I realise why we are late. We didn't make it. I realise what heaven, what a houri I have lost in such a short time. I cannot even manage to cry. A deep pain, as heavy as her dead body, sits on my chest, and I can hear my heart beating. My heartbeats hit my ribcage like a wooden pestle hits the mortar.

---

[18] Yezîdchilgîr: It is like a white kaftan which fasting Yazidi Kurds wear, They withdraw themselves from the world and devote themselves to praying and pious considerations.

I moan, I bleed inside, but not one teardrop comes down from my eyes. My eyes turn into uncultivable arid land and can produce no tears. I sigh deeply, and simultaneously I hear a sound like moaning behind me. I assume there is someone else around. I turn around, but there is no one there. I realise that it was an echo of my own sigh.

Mekrus effendi and the man with white kaftan have left me alone in here. I am on my own with the dead body if I don't count God. I mumble quietly to myself, as if I want to prevent someone else from hearing my voice as if I am hiding from someone. 'Come on! Get up and tell me, Nagina. I know that you have drawn the curtain of silence over yourself and you cannot and will never hear anything more. I know there won't be any sound coming from you anymore. As before, during our journey together, you will not tell me anything I want to hear. The spring we came across and stayed by was clear and clean. The mountain summits we climbed were not lower than Hira and Sinai. In other words, my passion was such that even God would come down and talk to me. But you didn't say a word. I know you didn't! I am going to say what I want to say: During that long journey when you were walking in front of me and I behind you, I made my feelings clear. You know it well, even if it was with few words. I opened my heart to you, I told you about my love, my passion for you.

'On the slopes of the mountains, by the rivers, under the full moonlight, we went into clean water naked. We made love. As you also know, you didn't say one single word. And now I know that it is too late and it is pointless to hope anymore. I have no hope of being able to hear a single word from you again. You acted like God. Yes, yes, you also did what God did to me – you turned your back on me. Everything has become cancerous in my eyes, in my heart, and in my soul. And I am plagued with questions. What is all this? Why did I fall in love with you? Why did you lead me, and why did we end up here? Why did you hide your real name, your real face, and your real life from me? Why did you stay silent and not say a word to me, Nagina? Although I am aware that my words are sinful, I have to say what is in my heart. I even told Mekrus effendi. Believe me, I loved you more that I loved God, Demora! That is the truth of my heart, and let those words be engraved in the sin book as a big sin of mine. And now, after this defeat, there is only one option left to me. I pray that the big sin I have committed will bring me an audience with God as a great sinner.'

And as a great sinner, I bend down on my knees in front of Nagina's body, lean my forehead against her perky breasts, and remain frozen in grief. I don't know how long I stay like that.

When the young man working at the gate calls me, he tells me that thirty-three moments have passed. I don't ask him what that means, but I do notice that his black hair and beard remain the same and have not turned grey. There are no wrinkles on his forehead, no dark rings under his eyes. He has not change or aged.

Without finding out about 'thirty-three moments', I rise from beside Nagina's body and walk out of the Castle of Silence. It is nearly dark outside. A wind colder than a breeze strokes my face, but I still can't make out how long I have been in there with Nagina. Mekrus effendi is waiting in front of the gate, sitting on the back of a black horse, as black as soot from a chimney. I assume he is waiting for me. I walk towards him and the soot-black horse. The horse is restless, chews the bit in his mouth, and fidgets. The steam from his funnel-like nostrils that rises and disappears into the air above his head looks like thick tobacco smoke. It makes me realise how cold it is.

I turn back for a moment as if I might gaze at Nagina one last time. I look at the Castle of Silence and the sky above it. It is evening and quiet. The twilight has taken over everywhere. Only the chimneys and the tower of the Castle of Silence are slightly distinguishable. I quietly approach the black horse and stop before it. I wait for Mekrus effendi either to say something or to lead me somewhere. However, he dismounts the soot-black horse, hands me the halter, and says: 'Don't stop! Ride! You have a long journey ahead of you. Ride and don't be late!'

I do not ask him what I will be late for, who is waiting for me, and why I am always on the move. At that moment I have only one thing on my mind, and you know as well as I do what that is: Nagina!

'Aren't you going to tell me what happened to Nagina? If they ask, what am I supposed to say, dear saint?'

'They know,' he says. 'Whoever knows her should know. No one is able to decide when they are born, but ehl-î-malê are able to decide their own death. They can decide to die from fire or the venom of a snake. It has always been like that and it will always be so. Don't forget.'

I engrave the information about ehl-î-malê in my mind so I won't forget. The words *snake* and *venom* remind me of the story about him and the snake.

I don't know why, or maybe without meaning it, I speak.

'Markus effendi,' I begin because I want to ask why in particularly he mentioned death by fire or the venom of a snake. I want to hear what His Holiness thinks about it. Before I manage to ask the question, I see how he is startled. He gives me such a look. How can I describe it? His eyes look as heavy as two millstones and as deep as two wells. I don't know whether it is because of this – the heaviness or deepness – but I am as quiet as he now. I still try to understand what I did, what I said or what happened to bring on this sadness in his eyes. He looks at me with a troubled expression.

'I wish you hadn't used that word,' he says. 'I wish you hadn't said *Markus*.'

I realise that I said *Markus* instead of *Mekrus* by mistake. I think about his piety, his strong faith, about his belief in Islam, and his village, Argon. I realise I must have called him by a non-Muslim name Markus, the name of one of the evangelists, and that is why he is startled and looks worried and sad. I apologize straight away.

'Forgive me, Mekrus effendi. Where I come from, they call non-Muslims *filleh* or *gawur*. Believe me, I didn't mean to be rude. It is just a habit from my education at the madrasa and that is why it just came out of my mouth like that. Your exalted person, I am Behram … Behram from Kawash, a student in the school of theology. At school, we learn about all religions, prophets, and holy books. And that name Markus is the name of one of Jesus' disciples. That is how it stayed in my mind. You will certainly know that our holy book tells about Prophet Jesus and Mary.[19] There is even a Mary surah consisting of ninety-eight holy verses

---

[19] Quran: Surah Mary, 19.

in the Quran. Please, being a good Muslim, don't get angry at me for calling you by a Christian name. As I said, this name has stayed in my mind from my studies. I didn't mean anything.'

After sighing deeply, he looks at me with the same sorrowful eyes.

'I know,' he says. 'No one can choose their own name when they are born, but this name ... My childhood name was Markus. After a calamity in my life, my name was changed from Markus to Mekrus and remained that way. After all this time, when you mentioned that name, it reminded me of that big, ill-omened calamity. It all came to life in front of my eyes again. The story of my name and my fate is long, a story that is as long as the length of a life.'

I don't know why, maybe to try to disperse his sorrow or to be forgiven, I say to him: 'I will listen. I want to hear your story, Mekrus effendi.'

'Listen,' he says, and he proceeds to relate one part of a very long story as we stand there.

These are the words of Mekrus effendi.

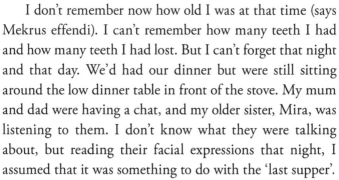

I don't remember now how old I was at that time (says Mekrus effendi). I can't remember how many teeth I had and how many teeth I had lost. But I can't forget that night and that day. We'd had our dinner but were still sitting around the low dinner table in front of the stove. My mum and dad were having a chat, and my older sister, Mira, was listening to them. I don't know what they were talking about, but reading their facial expressions that night, I assumed that it was something to do with the 'last supper'.

Late in the evening, there was a knock of the gate. As soon as my mother heard the knock, she lifted her hand up and down, left and right, making the sign of the cross. She looked up towards the ceiling as if the Messiah himself were there and she was hoping for help from him. My dad remained quite rigid. My sister's olive-skinned face turned white, as white as my father's Rizla. When there was a second knock on the door, my mum stood up and headed towards the gate. She must have got her strength from praying to the

Messiah. Her action must have reminded my dad that he was the man of the house, so he stood up as well. I can see it all so clearly still. Mira was buttoning her cardigan, as if she was hiding her newly-grown breasts from someone, and she followed my parents. I don't know why, but I also stood up. I rushed past everyone and reached the gate before them. My mum got hold of my flannel undershirt and pulled so hard that she wrenched me off my feet and into the air. I must have looked like a flying cherub.

Mumbling prayers, my mother made the sign of the cross again and reached out to the handle of the gate. At that moment my father put his hand on his scabbard and shouted: 'Who is it?'

Those few words ... those three words that are not even as long as one single word of other languages when put together, came out of his mouth in Kurmancî. My father didn't speak Turkish, nor did he speak Armenian. I don't know who he was expecting, what language he was expecting to hear, but the voice that answered behind the gate was in Kurmancî as well.

'It is I, *pismam*[20].'

With the mention of pismam, my mother released my flannel undershirt, and everyone exhaled. My father's Kurdish friends called him pismam. Although the man didn't tell his name, my father recognized his voice, and mother opened the gate.

My father's pismam was a Kurd from Argon, the village close to us. After my mother opened the gate and he came in, I realised that he had not arrived on horseback but had come on foot. He looked more worried and scared than my

---

[20] Male cousin.

father. I was still standing next to them in the garden when my father indicated that my mother and Mira should get the guestroom ready. I don't think I understood any of what was said other than the word *ferman*[21] during their conversation, but I could see from their expressions that the news was not good. I didn't know this word would bring disaster, pain, and sorrow with it. I had heard that word so many times in our house that I had learnt it by heart, which may be why I remember it. Not because I couldn't speak Kurdish. My Kurdish was better than the language we used for prayer since all my playmates in the village spoke Kurdish. Our family had good relation with Kurds, not only the Kurds in our village, but those in neighbouring villages too. As I said, the pismam who came was a Kurdish man from Argon.

As we went inside, I saw that there was no hope in my father's eyes. It was as if the whole world's burden was put in a sack and laid on his shoulders; as if the house was no longer his, and he couldn't be a host to his guest; as if he wanted to throw himself into bed and not wake up again. He was mortified. His shoulder slumped, and he suddenly had a hump. If the hump wasn't caused by the jacket he was wearing, I am sure it was caused by the weight of the word ferman that his pismam had come this late dark night to inform him about. With that weight on his shoulder, they stepped inside the guest room. After eating and drinking tea, my father's pismam stood up and got ready to leave. My mum put some scones she had made for Easter and colourful Easter eggs in a piece of cloth, made a knotted bundle, and gave it to him. Dad followed him to the gate to see him off.

---

[21] Imperial edict.

Dad's pismam rushed away into the darkness as rapidly as he had appeared earlier.

My sister Mira and I were left alone in the hall. After Dad's pismam left, Dad put his hand on Mum's shoulder, and they walked into the guest room and closed the door. Mira was quiet and looked sad. It was obvious that she couldn't look at me or talk to me. She was pensive, and she seemed to be thinking about everything and about nothing.

It was the first time Dad took Mum away from us and talked secretly, but they didn't stay away long. They came out of the guest room and stayed by the furnace. Dad's eyes were red, and Mum's eyelashes were wet as if she had an eyeliner of tears. She walked towards her trousseau chest with wet eyelashes. It was obvious that something was going on. I couldn't differentiate whether it was a party or mourning. Mum used to open her trousseau chest only on those two occasions. She kept her black mourning dress and her colourful party clothes in there. But this time, it was only my dad who was getting ready, not Mum. Everything indicated that this night was pregnant with some events – an inauspicious event that I wasn't aware of and didn't think to ask.

My dad put some warm clothes on. Instead of an Armenian hat, he put on a fur cap for snow weather and, like a Kurdish man, he tied a long scarf around his waist and pushed his "David" sword under it. He had named his sword David. His smart dress and finery and his tall, well-proportioned body made him look awesome and dreadful. My mum walked away from her trousseau chest towards my dad and put something in his pocket, trying to hide it from us.

My sister, Mira, stood up, still looking very sad. I was sure that my dad was going on a journey. I did what my sister did. I also stood up and walked towards my dad with calm steps, but with curiosity. Dad looked at me, looked at my sister … I don't know what he was thinking, but I could feel that at that moment he was wishing that we weren't his children. It was as if creating us was a big sin. No, no, not one sin; it was two big sins. That was how he was looking at me and Mira. With that sinful feeling, he opened his arms and stretched his hands towards me so that I would run and throw myself in his arms. I did so as always. Whilst I was in his arms, I realised that his throat was so tight and his eyes so full of tears that he couldn't talk. He *didn't* talk. His heart was full, his throat was full, and his eyes were full. I turned towards Mum whilst in Dad's arms and saw that she also had started to cry.

No one asked where Dad was going. But I think everyone except me knew about the *tofan*, about the violence and the wrath. Both of them knew. That is why they didn't ask. Dad walked towards Mira, embraced her hard, and we walked him to the gate. It was a pitch black night. Dad opened the gate, and then turned to Mum.

'*Bundan sonraki tufan nedir bilir misin, azizem?*'[22] he said and walked out. He became part of the dark night in the street and disappeared.

Mira and I couldn't speak Turkish. Mum understood a little, but whenever they wanted to say something secret, something they didn't want us to know, they used to speak Turkish together. I assume that Mum understood those words well, better than usual, so she drove us inside and

---

[22] Turkish: 'My beloved, you know very well what the next wrath is!'

followed us with wet eyelashes. I had heard crying in our house before, but not like this. Mum was crying more than Mira, but I didn't understand whether they were crying because Dad left or because of his last words.

Mum didn't do anything that night. She sat by the furnace. Mira sat in bed with the blanket on her shoulders all night. And I looked at the wooden logs supporting the ceiling for a long time.

I don't how much sleep any of us had. Cavalrymen reached our village before dawn. I heard voices of cursing before opening my eyes. When I opened my eyes and saw the condition of Mum and the house, I realised that the unpleasantness had reached our door. Mum's eyelashes were dry now. Maybe she didn't have any tears left after a night of crying, or maybe she was putting a brave face on. Maybe she was acting heroically as a result of helplessness, fear, and anger. She was rushing from one room to another, then running to the window or out of the door. She would face Saint Gevorg Church, placing a hand on her chest and making the sign of the cross as if she was calling for help from the Messiah. And as far as I remember now, she was praying and saying *'Astvadzim, tun yes mer miyag huyisi pirge anxixc, ankut martotsme!'*[23]

With those prayers on her lips, she brought some cloths to Mira and me. She wanted us to dress warm. Among those worn-out old clothes, I saw my dad's old coat. Mum wanted Mira to put on clothing like that in order to hide her beauty. But before Mira managed to cover even half her beauty, the cavalry men appeared outside and were banging loudly on

---

[23] Armenian: 'God! You are the only help. Please save us from those stony-hearted tyrants!'

the garden gate. Mira's eyes got bigger, which made her even more beautiful and more obviously feminine. Mum started to pray and curse, and shaking with fear, she headed towards the gate to open it. My sister and I followed her. As soon as mum opened the gate, the cavalry men stormed into the garden like dung flies.

I don't remember what my mother said or in which language she spoke, but I do remember one of them put a bayonet to her chest. Mum didn't attempt to remove the bayonet that was pushed between her breasts. Mira was standing behind my mum with her hands covering her mouth. God knows, she must have been expecting the worst. Suddenly, a cavalryman as stiff and tall as a mast came galloping into the courtyard from the other side of the street. Holding the horse's rein in one hand and a whip in the other, he gave a command to the soldiers in our garden and rode off. I don't know what he said, but all the soldiers got ready to leave.

Only one stayed behind, the one who placed his bayonet between Mum's breasts. He talked to Mum. I don't know what he told her, what they agreed about, but he stayed by the garden gate and Mum took us inside and informed us that we were going on a journey. She didn't tell us where we were going or where the journey would end. She only said: 'We are leaving the house and the village now. No one except God knows where.' But I knew that it was not only God who knew. Mum knew as well because she had made us provisions for a journey the night before.

Mum and Mira put the bags on their backs, and we left home. The cavalryman was still waiting for us outside the garden gate. When Mum put the padlock on the gate and locked it, tears were running down her cheeks, and she was mumbling to herself: *"Ayn tserki vor turis pana anitzal ila, godri, or cidesne, astutzime kidna!"*[24] When I heard those words, I was sure that Mum didn't know who would unlock her door.

Many travellers of this uncertain journey had already gathered around in the square behind Saint Gevorg's church. It was obvious that we were the last ones to join in. All Armenians, in other words all infidels – all non-Muslims were called *filleh*[25] by the Muslim people in the village – had gathered or been collected together by force. There were no men other than some old and ill ones in the assembly. All the fit men had left. Only women, children, and old, ill men had stayed behind.

The cavalrymen had surrounded them like hyenas. Besides the cavalrymen surrounding them, some soldiers had intruded in the crowd. Like cattle merchants looking for fat and meaty sheep at a cattle fair, like brothel keepers, they were eying the girls and young brides.

A straight-mast-looking cavalry man on horseback took his gun out and aimed the barrel towards God in the church bell. At that moment, smoke came out of the barrel of the gun with a horrible sound. No one moved or reacted except for some children who screamed. Everyone was quiet. 'Straight-mast' then started to say something, and those who understood what he said translated for those who didn't. 'He says whoever resists will be killed.' No one wanted to

---

[24] Armenian: 'May those hands that open this door have no luck in life. May their hands break, and may they not be able to see the daylight!'
[25] Infidels.

be killed, so no one disobeyed. Then the soldiers who were moving among us started to threaten the young women, and the cry and scream of the young virgins mixed with their mothers' moaning and cursing.

Some of the soldiers were pulling girls and brides with breasts inside the church. God knows, they wanted to do bad things to those girls and brides in God's house in the presence of Saint Gevorg. I could clearly see the position my mother was facing. She felt that she needed to protect Mira more than me. She didn't want to leave Mira alone. In that state of mind, she slipped her hand inside her bodice and took a gold-coloured holy crucifix out from between her breasts. She bent her head over me, put the laceless cross inside my palm, and whispered in my ear.

'When you get an opportunity, run, Markus. Run and go to Lady Damina's house. Don't be afraid. She will help you, and she will tell you how to get away.'

I didn't understand what Mum meant at the time. I didn't understand whether it was the holy cross in the palm of my hand or Lady Damina who would help me and show me a way out of this. Whilst I was puzzling over this, I suddenly realised that my mother was shaking a soldier by the collar. He was short and chubby. He was trying to pull Mira away from Mum. Mum didn't want anything to happen to Mira while she was alive. She didn't want her daughter to die before her. She was fighting to prevent Mira from being taken away by the soldier. She had become like a strong, high wall for she was tall. When the soldier tried to hit Mum with his bayonet, Mum gave him such a hard slap on the face that he fell on the ground with his gun in front of her feet.

All hell broke loose after Mum slapped the soldier. Holy Gevorg's square turned into the square of the *Mahşer*[26]. It looked like doomsday to me – all that violence that erupted after Mum's slap.

Mothers were using their long dresses as wings in order to hide and protect their children and babies. They thought that their long skirts were steel shields and the bayonets would not get through. They were shouting imprecations and crying for help from the Messiah. To me it sounded as if God had poured all the suffering that was left over from the square of Golgotha onto the Armenians in our village. God had chosen them for suffering.

When I realised that God had a hand in all that suffering and punishment of those people, I ran from the gathering in utter confusion and headed towards Lady Damina's house.

Lady Damina is the daughter of a Kurdish Mîr[27] and wife of the head of the Cemaldîn tribe. She liked my mum very much. When she saw me in her courtyard, she ran towards me, grabbed my hand quickly, and pulled me inside the house. Inside, she bent over me like an angel with wings. She put some of her children's old clothes on me, and when she selected one of those white Muslim praying caps, I remembered my cross – the cross that Mum had put in the palm of my hand in the middle of the violence – and I clutched it. Lady Damina saw the cross. She slowly took it from me with shaking hands and a worried expression, looked at me with wet eyes, and said: 'Do not leave this house or the garden. I will find a nice string to put your cross on so you can hang it on your neck.'

---

[26] The last judgement.
[27] Lord.

I didn't say anything. I didn't mind giving Mum's cross to her. I did as I was told. I didn't go out of Lady Damina's garden for a few days.

They told me later on that lots of people were killed during the tumult in the square behind Saint Gevorg's Church. They buried all the dead bodies together in a big hole without the church bells ringing, without a ceremony, without grieving or crying. Those who were alive and wounded, those who survived the killing, were taken away by the soldiers on a journey that would lead to nowhere except death.

The only survivors in my family were my cross and me. We were staying at Lady Damina's house. In order to hide it and to prevent people from noticing it, she covered my cross in a green cloth like an amulet which looks like a sign of Islam from outside, with its triangle shape, and a recognition of Christianity on the inside with its cross. But I don't think either of us did this because of our beliefs, but for Mum's sake.

For the sake of Mum, every time Lady Damina served me food, she prayed in the name of the tombs and places of saints and the prophets that God would punish the guilty ones to right the wrongs of those who were suffering.

But nothing helped to make any impression on God, and he never granted the right of the suffering ones over those who were guilty. There was no news whatsoever of Mum and Mira. Until today, there has never been the slightest trace of them and my dad. I still don't know when, where, and how they placed their foreheads in the cold earth. It is said that no one knows. And those who know about what happened interpreted everything to be divine fate, acts of God.

The acts of God have taught me pain. I learned how it feels to lose my mum and my dad, how it hurts when one loses an older sister, how the pain makes one rebel against the saints. That is what made me a rebel.

I become disappointed in the Messiah. I looked coldly at God. I realised that they were not beneficial to me. I learned that there is no such a place as hell. Hell is just circumstances like what occurred behind the Saint Gevorg church. In such a hell, no one calls to God and asks for mercy. In such a hell, one hates God for creating human beings and making tyrants out of them.

And so, just as there is no difference between for a man who is drunk to sleep with his own wife or another random woman, for me there was no difference between religions any more. To be honest, I no longer had any religious belief. In other words, all I had left were the calves. I was a herdsman for calves. Calves were my hope, my belief, my prophet, my God.

After a time, my father's cousin came, the one who came in secret to our house after our last dinner in our home that last night to inform us about the ferman and violence that was on the way. He liked me a lot, and I liked him and got very fond of him. He was the one who guided and helped me and made me like snakes, the one who left everything he owned to me when he left this world. He came to Lady Damina's house, talked to her, and took me with him to his village to live with him. From that day, I became a herdsman for my dad's pismam in the village of Argon.

It must have been for the sake of my father that his pismam didn't try or want to change my name. He kept my original name, Markus. The name Markus fell out of use when I was herding cattle in the village of Argon among the Muslim inhabitants. It got changed to Mekrus and spread all over the world as Mekrus. In other words and briefly said, the name of Markus, being one of the Messiah's disciples, was changed into Mekrus, the name of the chief demon. I know God is not pleased that my name is Mekrus, but I am.

◆————＊◆＊————◆

'What did you say your name is?' Mekrus effendi asks.

'Behram ... Behram from Kawash,' I say, but after hearing the story of his life, I don't say 'Behram from Kawash, a student from the school of theology' any more. God knows, after hearing the story of his life, I feel ashamed of the name of the school of theology, and I feel ashamed to be a student of theology. That is why I don't say it. For the knowledge of theology that I was learning, he had experienced himself. He had experienced the truth directly. As an Armenian, he had faced the book of life – a life without joy and goodness, a life without any help and mercy from prophets and their Lord.

Like Mekrus, I start to doubt the prophets as well as God and become distanced from them, start to lose desire for them. I want to know more about it, but I realise how deeply he is hurt and how the pain has resurfaced when he talked about it, and that stops me from asking him further questions. However, Mekrus effendi continues to talk himself.

'Behram from Kawash, student of the school of theology, some learn by studying, some learn by seeing, and some learn by living. And out of those people, some believe, some people get scared, and some understand,' he says. He puts his hand on my shoulder and points to the darkness of the night. 'That is the way of truth. If you want to know the truth, do not stray from the direct route. If you feel unsure which route to take during your journey, listen to your heart and keep going. Feelings that rise to the surface along the shore are a sign of the right direction, the right journey, a journey that every good person has to take, a road that every good person has to walk along. You are going to learn everything during this journey – everything you want to know. You are going to witness everything.'

To be able see everything, I make the soot-black horse gallop and head towards the darkness. I get away from the Castle of Silence, from Mekrus effendi, from Nagina and her body. A pain as heavy as her body weighs on my heart and makes me realise that I am not going to see her anymore. I am sure of it. Other than that, I don't know what I am going to face and witness during the journey. I don't know where I am heading. The rocks and trees on the left and right sides of the road look like a herd of bulls running past me on both sides, and I become part of the darkness and disappear into it.

As if the soot-black horse knows its way, I loosen the harness, and we get caught by the wind. He lifts his head up and bends it backward as if guarding my chest. His mane is flying across my chest like a shield from the strong wind. The smell of his sweat overwhelms me. I leave my fate to his cleverness, his loyalty.

All the mountains and lakes I ride past on my way, all the cottages and tents I see in the distance ... everything seems so strange to me. Not even in my dreams have I seen such places. There is no sign of a mosque or church that can make the place familiar so that I feel that I have been here or lived here before. The place seems to be uninhabited, the road is empty, and the time is empty. It is a desolated place, a desolated road, and a desolated time.

I don't know how long the journey takes, but the darkness of the night is in charge all over. I reach the slope of a mountain. A fire is visible far away. I head towards the fire. I think it is a caravanserai. The road that the soot-black horse and I are riding on leads directly to the caravanserai, and I realise that the soot-black horse has been to this caravanserai many times before. As I get closer, it appears like a big structure surrounded by high walls. It looks like a fortress. The dome of the fortress looks like a white goblet. The fire, which was visible from far away, is glowing in the garden inside the fortress. It sounds as if there is a party or mourning going on in the garden. I can hear voices. It sounds like voices of women, men, and children. They are all mixed. I am still confused. I don't know whether it is a caravanserai or a fortress. The guard in front of the big gate with a girdle pattern lifts his lantern and makes a sign for me to go there. And I do so. I ride my horse towards the big girdle-patterned gate. I assume that it must be one of the on-duty guards of the fortress.

But as I get closer, I realise that the guard has not got a sword, a shield, or a spear. I dismiss the thought that this is a fortress there.

'Good morning, you good and noble person,' I say.

'You are welcome, you good-mannered man,' he says.

'May God increase your good manner and welcome! Where is this place? Will you accept an unexpected guest?'

'This is the land of ehl-î-malê,' he says. 'To us it is a sin to welcome and shelter guests. Here in this land, there is only one place to welcome and treat guests with marks of respect and distinction, and that is the house of the great leader.'

The words *great leader* reminds me immediately of the words of Mekrus effendi, and I get confused and wonder if the guard means Satan. But I don't ask him. I don't ask the question for the sake of all the other highnesses and princes. It is not appropriate to ask who the great leader is.

Because it is a sin to be welcomed and sheltered by other member other than the great leader, I say: 'Excuse me for troubling you, but please guide me to the house of the great leader.'

'With pleasure!' he says. 'But there is an act of worship going on right now. When that finishes, I will take you. That is my duty.'

When I dismount, the dutiful guard – well aware of his duties – takes hold of the halter, leads the soot-black horse under a tree, and ties the halter to one of the branches. He then returns and shows me the stone staircase and invites me to go up. He does so in a respectful manner, gesturing 'after you'. As we walk up the stairs, he tells me that the place is a temple. We sit in the bastion of the temple at the top. The inside of the tower looks like a fairy tale room, with its colourful patterned rugs and woven wool matting. According to the guard, I have to wait here until the ceremony ends. And I wait.

From up here, I can see the inside of the temple courtyard. A big fire is rising in the middle. Everyone – old and young, women and men, big and small children – has circled the fire. As they walk round, they chant to the heart breaking music of tambourines and cymbals. I don't hear the words of their prayers, but the melody of their act of

worship is so touching, so sad, so heart breaking. It is the
kind of sound that exists only in Kurdish songs. The women
and girls are half-naked. They are naked from the breasts up
and from the thighs down. The way they dance around the
fire catches my attention more than their nakedness. They
spin around their own axes, spin round one another and
circle the fire, all in time to the words and music. They are
all barefoot – and I suddenly realise that I am also barefoot.
I take it that this is to do with the holiness of the place.

I turn to the guard and say: 'What is this ceremony for?
Is it in honour of a special day?'

He says: 'This is an act of worship for defence ... defence
and multiplication. After this ceremony, all virgin boys and
girls will go to the high plateau ... this high holy plateau.
They will get to know each other, they will smell each other,
and they will make love with each other in order to multiply.'

I don't understand very much from the words of the
guard, but I don't want to ask too many questions in case
I upset him. I worry that I may say something contrary to
his culture, something that is inappropriate to this place
and to this land.

After the ceremony, the prayers, and the dance around
the fire, I see an old man climbing onto a high platform
surrounded and decorated with lanterns. He is old, but he
doesn't have a walking stick. The guard tells me that he is
the spiritual man of the ehl-î-malê. He has long hair, a long
beard, and a long moustache. He places his right hand on his
heart and stretches his left hand towards the fire as if he is
going to take an oath. Every word of his incantation is loud
and clear. His words are so clear and so loud that I can hear
them from the bastion of the temple where I sit.

After every sentence, the entire ehl-î-malê around the fire repeat his words.

The wise old man declaims:

> [1]It is said
> Moses has taken his tribe and led them into the Red Sea.
> We have gone in front of our people,
> And climbing our mountains
> And taking cover in our high plateau.
> Our high plateaus
> Are as big as the patience of the gods.

All of ehl-î-malê repeat with one voice: Our high plateaus are as big as the patience of the gods.

> [2]At ours
> Around here
> The worthiness of God and the Great Leader
> Is of the same colour
> And the same voice.
> One is not better than the other.

All of ehl-î-malê repeat with one voice: One is not better than the other.

> [3]Until now
> Either ill meant
> Or good meant
> We have not said anything about anything.

All of ehl-î-malê repeat it with one voice: We have not said anything about anything.

> [4]Without goodness,
> Without badness,
> From the old times till now,
> With the effort
> And the sweat,
> We have taken the plough rod in our hands.
> Walking behind the pair of bulls and behind buffalos,
> We have dug the black soil.
> We planted the seed
> So that we can harvest food for our children.

All of ehl-î-malê repeat with one voice: We plant the grain so we can harvest food for our children.

> [5]Years of dearth and famine have visited us.
> Severe epidemics have depleted us.
> War,
> Fire,
> Death,
> Severe disasters have befallen us,
> And the pain and sorrow of life
> Have drawn deep lines in our foreheads.
> As deep as valleys and inlets of this holy land
> Have the lines stretched.
> Yet we have not opened our hands and begged,
> Nor have we asked for anything.

All of ehl-î-malê repeat with one voice: We have not opened our hands and begged, Nor have we asked for anything,

> [6]As if this pain and suffering were not enough.
> Furthermore,
> Our land has been occupied by people
> Whose language we do not even know.

All of ehl-î-malê repeat with one voice: Whose language we do not even know,

> [7]Those whose language we do not know.
> Those ill-meaning pillagers
> With the power of sharp swords
> And the strength of the mace
> With the power of religion,
> With the words of scriptures,
> With the books of God
> They attacked us
> Because we are not ehl-î-kitêb

All of ehl-î-malê repeat with one voice: We are not ehl-î-kitêb.

> [8]Those people
> In the bold and dried deserts
> Riding on the backs of camels
> On the knees of the camels,
> With made-up words they lined up
> Which they want to make
> As a rule for us
> As a religion for us,

As a belief for us,
Words that are as straight as the hump and the neck
of their camels.

All of ehl-î-malê repeat with one voice: Words that are
as straight as the hump and the neck of their camels.

[9]The possessors of such word and actions
Have planted our ancestors' bones
In those high plateaus.
And today we water it with our children's blood
During our lives
In our lands
With pain we have always been planted.
With dead we have been harvested.
It is obvious even from our meadows
That all our memories have been covered.
All our pain has been hidden.
No one ever knew it
Except God.

All ehl-î-malê repeat with one voice: No one ever knew
about it except God.

[10]Once upon a time
In our land
On our high plateaus,
The shadow of every rock
Would protect us like the power of thirty-three
Gods.
But now,
Even around here,

After all the ill omen,
Impossible to live,
To live without a God and prophets.

All of ehl-î-malê repeat with one voice: No possibility of life to live without a God and prophets.

[11]And now down here
On the slopes of this holy mountain,
We have raised pillars,
Put the tents up,
Tightened the ropes,
Placed a fence around it all
To be able to be rooted and settled
Since we have no other place or land
Except this land to settle.
Taking refuge with Your protection
We will not leave our land

All of ehl-î-malê repeat with voice: We will not leave our land.

[12]We are waiting
We hope
That Your Excellency
Makes a book
From our beliefs,
From our thoughts
From our and his words
In our language
To guide us,
To protect us.

All of ehl-î-malê repeat with one voice: To guide us, to protect us.

After all that ceremony and prayers, all the ehl-î-malê walk away from the fire and leave the courtyard. All virgin boys and girls walk towards the high plateaus, and the ones who are left disperse towards their tents and cottages.

Only Derpiro, the temple guard, and I are left. That is when he tells his name. Derpiro points again towards the stone stairs, inviting me to go down from the tower. I do so. We both go down. We leave the soot-black horse behind, in front of the temple, and walk upward towards the north. We are directing our steps towards the house of the Great Leader, whose greatness I can only guess at.

I ask Derpiro: 'Is there anyone greater than the Great Commander here?'

Derpiro suddenly turns towards me and answers. 'There is no one and nothing greater than the Great Commander, not around here or anywhere else.'

I think to myself: God knows best, so he must be the Great Commander himself. According to Mekrus effendi, this one must be the one who has many names, the one we all have been taught about with the different adjectives and symbols.

We leave.

Derpiro and I leave the tower and the temple behind. We reach a big rock on the top of a hill. It is not far from the temple. Derpiro names the rock for Aridora. It is wider than a cathedral and taller than a minaret. It looks as if during ancient times, rain, snow, and wind eroded the soil of the top of the hill and left this huge ancient rock behind. The path curls to the southeast of the rock and then directs us to the north. There is a door on the north side of the rock, which is as big as a Buddha statue. The big stone that covers the door like a belt has been embroidered with the pattern of snakes and the head of wild goats. Before going inside, Derpiro turns to me.

'This is the house of the Great Commander,' he says and walks inside in front of me.

I am more curious about what the Commander looks like than about his name and fame, and I am not scared. Rather, I am excited. I am nervous in the way a newly-married couple might be on entering their nuptial chamber.

We enter a big hall, which is lit by a fire. The first thing that catches my attention is the fire for it has no smoke. Derpiro explains that it has always been like that and it will always be like that. Further up in the hall, there is a fireplace that looks like a tandoor or furnace burning. The flames of the fire have overtaken the hall light. They create a warm and cosy atmosphere. I see a shadow sitting in front of the furnace. Its owner sits like a great leader and commander. He watches the fire quietly and without moving. His head and face are covered with a watery-blue silky cloth.

The way he is sitting, the stillness and quietness, and his facial covering all suggest that he must be a great mystic leader. Only great savants who are close to God act like this. They attempt to be closer to God by being on their own in silence.

And yet Derpiro walks calmly and steadily up to him, bows like a disciple, and says, 'Your Exalted Person, you have a visitor. Beloved saint, you have a guest.' Then, with the same respectful attitude, he steps backward and leaves the hall. He leaves us alone. I am on my own in the presence of the Great Commander – he and I, on our own. Whilst standing there, I expect, like everyone else, to see a crooked face, horns, and a tail. I expect to see Satan with billy goat hooves. I don't know how and why, but I am not the slightest bit afraid. I don't have any fear. The fear that could trick me, seduce me, take me off track, throw me into the fire of hell and hurt me was far away from me. I reason that, if my lack of fear is not due to the holy sanctification ceremony Mekrus effendi was talking about, it must then be due to my coming too close to the Great Commander. That must be why I have no sign of fear. The distance between him and me is no longer than an ox goad. The thought of being able to see the beloved saint's face makes my heart beat faster and my blood warmer.

When he slowly lifts the silky woven cloth with both hands, I see his face. How can I describe it? It is as if that the face has been created, not by the hands of God, but by the hands of Leonardo da Vinci. I will never forget that face, a form that I will never see repeated. I see an angel that looks like a human. He doesn't look like a ruler or judge. He makes me think of a good dervish, a good hermit who has been living on sweet fruit juice and raisins. He is good-looking – *very* good-looking. His light brown hair hangs over his shoulders in a few plaits. When he looks at me, his eyes emanate a special, pure warmness that envelops me.

He doesn't turn his whole body and look directly at me as a prophet would do, but eyes me softly over his shoulder. His expression is full of sorrow and tenderness, and his lips seem to speak knowledge, anxiety, happiness, pain, trouble, hatred, uneasiness. All of these are reflected in his face, and none of those features are more superior or prominent than any other. It is difficult to distinguish whether he is happy or sad. He has got long and white fingers that remind me of fingers of a princess. It makes me think that there are no bones in his fingers.

There is one difference from Leonardo da Vinci's drawings: It is difficult to decide whether it is a man or a woman. I get confused. I don't know how to address this being: whether to call 'him' prince or princess. It is indeterminate. Whilst I am wondering how to act and talk in this enchanted situation, he says, 'Welcome! Welcome with all goodness.'

'Thank you,' I reply. 'May God's kindness and goodness be with you.'

I don't use the word *God* for religious reasons or because I desire to be religious, nor is it my fear of God that moves me to do so. Maybe it is simply due to habit that the word *God* came out of my mouth. With that, he smiles at me. I don't know if the smile is because of uneasiness or something else.

At that moment I recall the conflict between him and God: that he is a rebellious angel, that he is God's enemy, that he is trying to derail human beings and cause them to burn in hellfire. And many other things that all the holy books have taught me about him. These thoughts suddenly come into my mind, and I say nothing. I no longer feel ashamed of the words 'kindness and goodness of God'. I'm not afraid that he might rise, insult me, harm me, make me suffer, and burn me in the fire. I don't know why, but God knows best. It must be down to his extraordinary, faultless being that I am not scared.

It suddenly becomes clear that the commander's voice doesn't match his name. His figure doesn't match his name. His appearance, his manner, and his style don't match his name. All the descriptions of his wicked actions, and his image that is known all over the world don't match him at all. To me it feels as if all those bad images and names have been imposed on him. Some sly tricksters have imposed all these bad images on him to deceive foolish people. I am in his presence right now, and I can see with my own eyes that he has no horn or tail as it was said he has. I now doubt all those names he has been given. I cannot believe that those bad actions could come from such a personality, that all those sins emanate from such a person. I get more suspicious, and I wait. I am still waiting for his comments about 'the kindness and goodness of God'.

But he says: 'Tell me, what good wind has blown you to this land and made you our guest?'

'May the goodness of the wind always be with you, Your Exalted Person!'

It must be because of his faultless appearance that the words 'Your Exalted Person' come out of my mouth. His glance, his elegance, his way of talking makes it difficult to hide my sympathy for him. I feel that I am becoming attached to him. On the other hand, my head feels heavy from all the questions and confusion in my mind. I am aware of the chaos in my head, and, God knows, maybe that is why I don't know what to say, how to answer his question. I don't know what good wind has blown me and made me a guest here.

'Master,' I say, 'I don't know where to start. To cut the long story short and not give you an unnecessary headache, I will start from my thirst.

'I felt thirsty. I asked Nagina for water. Nagina is my landlord's daughter, but I found out that she is known as Demora in these lands. Demora went, and I followed her. She walked in front of me, and we started off to search for water. She and I travelled a long way together, and we came together. But somewhere on the road, during our journey, we lost each other. Well, maybe I lost her. Then I met Mekrus effendi, who is her grandfather. During the journey, there were a lot of things that I wanted to know and understand, but Mekrus effendi didn't tell me. He just gave me the reins of a soot-black horse and said: "If you want to know the Truth, you need to set off on this journey, on this road. It is the way to knowledge and truth. Do not deviate until you reach your destination."

'I did as he said. I did not go off the track till I reached here. I have come on my own unless you count the soot-black horse accompanying me. And regarding who I am – I am Behram from Kawash, a student in the school of theology.'

When I finish talking, the Great Commander reaches slowly for a jug on his left side, fills two silver cups, hands one of them to me, and says, 'Here you are, Behram from Kawash, the student of the school of theology.'

And I, as Behram from Kawash, student of the school of theology, honoured by his presence, take the cup from the Great Commander, in other words, from the hands of Satan. I don't remember the taste, the colour, or the clearness of the drink. But if it was somewhere else, another time, if it was offered to me by someone else, I swear I would be suspicious, and I would not have taken it and drunk it. But because I feel very close to him, and find him very warm-hearted, I don't hesitate. I drink. He drinks. We drink together. I still don't know what that drink was. After the drink, I feel very relaxed, as if my inner and outer being have been cleaned and made one.

I put the empty cup down where His Honour has placed the jug and the cups.

'Please sit down,' he says. 'Sit and tell me what you want from me.'

I sit on something in front of him, but I cannot remember what it was. He is so soft, so warm, and so sweet with his look, with his manner, with his words, that one can trust him totally. He gives one confidence. I realise that I like him, and I am happy with him, and I feel he likes me as well. I wonder why such an angel, the angel of all angels and such a great person, has been given such a bad reputation.

'I want to know, sir!' I say firmly.

'What do you want to know?'

'Everything. I want to know what this place is. Why did Nagina guide me here? Why am I on this journey? Why is your name considered bad? I want to know. I want to know the story of everything.'

I ask the Great Commander to tell me everything because I know that I am going to learn a lot from him, all those things that have become a headache for me, that have become a hope, things that have filled my heart with good and bad feelings. I am curious as to how he will react to my request.

He slowly reaches for the stick next to him and stirs the fire. The embers emit sparks. The sparks rise and reach the ceiling before going out. Suddenly, a warm and harmonic shiver overtakes my entire body, and I start looking all around me for no reason. I see now that the inside of the Great Commander's house reminds me of the shape and colour of a big old ship, like an old Viking ship.

I realise that my eyes have only just attuned to the darkness of the house. This awareness happens while he is stirring the fire. I look at His Excellency with surprise, as if it is the first time I see this panorama, and I make clear to him how happy I am with him, with his house, with his greatness, with his kindness, and with his understanding. He turns to me with his kind, warm, and friendly expression and continues.

'This land is the place of your heart. It is the place where your heart wants to be. The journey and Nagina are simply the instruments to allow this to happen. Knowledge is sinful. And to know everything is the greatest sin. And this greatest sin is mine.'

I say nothing, though I am not tense or scared. I wait for him – the greatest sinner – to tell me himself, and I want to listen to him.

'God has named me the greatest sinner. But he is a bigger sinner than I am. I told him this long ago. I told him without hesitation that he was the biggest sinner himself. But he didn't take any notice. He did what he wanted to do. He did as he wanted, and he used me for his sins and labelled me with that name.'

Hearing these words of his, I realise that I have been granted a magical treasure. I have discovered a book from time immemorial, a book that until now has been unknown as to purpose, content and authorship. I am quite sure now that I am in the presence of the Great Commander, the greatest angel and the well-known Satan himself in a different place and in a different time. God has ordered human beings to tell the truth, and I am telling the truth: At that moment, I do not think to take God's side and to start a holy war against the biggest sinner. It is not because I am scared. No, even God knows that. It is only because of my curiosity and my uncertainty. I feel a strong uncertainty, and I feel curious about the truth of everything.

'In our land,' I say, 'we talk badly of you. We associate you with wickedness. That is what we have been told, that is what we have learnt, and that is what we know.' I include myself as well, being one of those people who associate his name with badness.

He replies: 'I know you all speak badly of me. You all think I am the evil one, and that I am the water and the flour of wickedness. But the truth is different. I am simply the scapegoat.'

'I beg Your Excellency to explain.'

The cause of all wickedness is the sons and daughters of Adam. It is their nature to listen to someone and believe what they are told. That is the reason, but that is a long story.'

'I am ready to listen,' I say. 'I have listened to many stories. I want to listen to the truth of this long story from you as well. I want your exalted person to tell me the story from the beginning.'

I ask him with all cordiality and sincerity, and there is no doubt about it. God knows, His Excellency Satan must have seen it from my face and voice, so he looks at me with a sincere, friendly, and warm-hearted expression like mine. His Excellency Satan regards me warmly.

'The beginning of the story: Darkness. Light. Earth. Sky. Water. Soil. Tree. Grass. Vermin. Everything, but without human beings. It was like that in the beginning. Our relationship, mine and God's, was very good in the beginning. Indeed it is still good, since God and I are like Siamese twins. We liked each other very much, and I think we still do. But all those things, the things that you and the sons and daughters of Adam have heard and seen, things you all have learnt and you are teaching, things you all know and that make you drown in pain, things you live with and make others live with, things that make you deceive and become deceived – all these things make the story.'

'What story?'

'The holy story, the story that everyone lives for and dies for. Your story, the story of existence, the creation of the sons and daughters of Adam. This story may be new to you, for the sons and daughters of Adam, but it is very old to me. It is as old as God and I. I begged him so much not to create the human beings from a handful of soil. Oh, how much I tried to talk him round, but it was no use! He still did as he wanted in the end. God did as he wanted.'

And now, the Great Commander does what he wants, too. He tells me the holy ancient story about the creation of human beings, the story of himself and God.

These are the words of Satan himself.

As I said (he began), after the beginning, after the creation, existence, and maturation of the universe, God called me one day and said 'Y' Ahriman'.

His Excellency God used to call me Ahriman. When he was happy and satisfied with his work and creations, his tongue would get heavy, and he would cut out some letters. His Excellency was using the letter Y in front of Ahriman to show reverence and respect. He meant to call me Ya Ahriman. Literally, the word $Y\bar{a}$ means O. It is a vocative signifying a direct address to a person.

I stood up with respect and said: 'Yes, Your Honour!'

God said: 'I am going to create something new now.'

I said: 'What are you going to create?'

God said: 'I am going to create a human being from the soil as a copy of myself.'

'Why?'

'For me.'

I kept quiet for the sake of his greatness. And he created Adam from the soil for himself. And long after, one day he came to me and said:

'Y' Ahriman!'

I realised he was happy and satisfied with his miracle work and was about to create something again. I stood up and said:

'Yes Your Honour!'

'And now I am going to create Eve.'

'Why is that?'

'For myself. Because I want to. I want Lady Eve to be with Adam. I want them to make love to each other. I want them, together with their sons and daughters, to see and witness all my miraculous works.'

'It is clear that Your Honour is adding children to their existence.'

He answered me happily and proudly as the greatest of the great masters.

'Yes, that is what I am going to do. I am going to make them able to reproduce and multiply so they can all see my miraculous works in the universe and benefit from them. Every time they taste, every time they use my inventions, they will be happy. When they are happy, they will bow down and worship me.'

'I don't get it.'

'What is it you don't get?'

'Adam is created from soil and manure. It is not going to work.'

He was disturbed by my words and turned to me with annoyance. 'I can create from the soil, from manure and from nothing if I want to. I say "soil", but when you add "manure", you belittle me.'

I felt sorry for His Greatness, but I didn't let him know.

'*Istaxfirellah!*[28]. Not at all! I mean the creation of human beings from soil will bring deficiency and lopsidedness. They will become handicapped and faulty human beings and nothing else. Imperfect human beings will produce faulty thoughts, faulty works, deficient souls, faulty appraisals, faulty stories, faulty words …'

He didn't let me finish and started to praise me.

'Bravo! You said "faulty". Those human beings I created are my copies. They are not me. My copy needs to be faulty and unfinished. In fact, that is the difference between the human beings and me. I have just donated one of my hundred names to Adam: *human being*. They are ninety-nine numbers less than me in the ranking. From the hundred, human beings know only ninety-nine of my names and images. But the last-ranking grade is my hidden side, which will remain as a mystical, concealed secret.'

'And?' I said, and waited for him to tell me more.

God continued.

'The aim of human beings will be to reduce the distance between them and me and try to become more like me during their lifetime. They have to reduce those ninety-nine grades of names by their belief and faith, with their words and actions, with their feelings and thoughts. The more they diminish, the closer they will become to me.'

I repeated:

'I don't get it. If I don't understand it, Adam and his sons and daughters will not understand either. They will

---

[28] I ask pardon of God!

not understand why they have been created. They will not understand the reason for their existence. All those hindrances, difficulties, and rankings Your Honour is placing in front of them. It will become like an unknown equation, which they will never be able to solve. It is impossible!'

'That is exactly what I mean by the mystery, which is the reason for my masterwork. They are not supposed to understand. Things that are understandable or solvable will lose their worthiness and their magic. I will ensure that they cannot understand the reason for their existence during their whole lifetime. I want them to search for an answer, to search for me, day and night, with every step they take and every breath that they breathe. I will make certain that they will never be cognizant of the mystery.'

'I am afraid that your secret will turn into a question amongst them. It will make them search for the answer. They will look for you, but they will also look in different directions, look for other greatness. All this will make them suffer. They will get hurt and kill each other and make Your Honour angry.'

God said angrily:

'Greatness is a name that belongs only to me. Greatness is my specificity alone.'

I said:

'*Amentubillah!*[29] There is no doubt. I do not question your greatness. I attach the same meaning to this word. Greatness belongs only to great ones. But greatness among the untaught sons and daughters of Adam is dangerous. If they don't get to know the reason for their existence, they

---

[29] I believe in God alone, who has no associate!

won't be able to recognise their own size and boundaries, which will make them pretend to be great to each other. If the feeling of being greater than another gets to human souls, it will create uneasiness and cause them to act wickedly. I am afraid that their greed to become greater will cause such harm that it cannot be named, even in today's divine language.'

This made God even angrier.

'If any human being tries to pretend to be great, I will dig his eyes out!'

'That is exactly what I am worried about. Why do you create them only to dig their eyes out?'

He pushed out his chest and said:

'I am the truth, I am the greatest. I am the creator. My creatures have to search for it and find it. The sons and daughters of Adam have to admire and worship my work and wonders. They have to see the truth.'

'If they don't see the truth, if they don't realise your greatness, Your Excellency?'

God repeated his threats.

'I will dig their eyes out. I will blind them and paralyze them. I will pour my divine wrath on them.'

'Isn't that a crime, Your Honour?'

God got angry and offended.

'What crime? Don't ask me questions. Questions make me uneasy.'

'If Your Honour is troubled, then don't do it. Don't create human beings, don't make them multiply, and don't make one better than the other. Those human beings you are creating will one day ask thousands of questions. Thereafter you will get angrier and will be more troubled.'

'I have created all this beauty in the universe for them. I want them to taste it and enjoy it.'

'Do it your own way! But be aware that all that enjoyment is not worth all their pain. Their health and happiness is not worth your trouble, Your Honour, because they will turn around one day and say: "The entire world is not worth one single tear of a child."[30]'

My words angered God still further.

'Don't tell me what to do! Don't teach me what to do! Don't get involved, and don't stir things up! I know what I am doing. I know things that you don't know. I am the one who knows, who can. I am the one who sees and makes what is going to happen. Everything is in my hands because I am the greatest.'

'If one day the sons and daughters of Adam are able to find out the story of their existence, that you have created them and everything for yourself, for your name and greatness, they will think the same as me. They will realise that their enjoyment is not worth their suffering. They will realise that no days of their life are worth even a short time of pain. Then they will become rebellious against everything, including themselves, and they will curse: "A curse on the day of my birth: let there be no blessing on the day when my mother had me. A curse on the man who gave the news to my father, saying, you have a male child; making him very glad."[31] Moreover, when they feel that way, they will not believe you anymore. The sons and daughters of Adam will deny you. They will distance themselves from you and your divine miraculous works.'

---

[30] F. Dostoyevski.
[31] Bible: Jeremiah 20:14,15.

This time God was beside himself with anger.

'Don't you dare make mischief! If you don't guide them, if you don't tell them, if you don't drive them off course, they will not be aware of these things, and they will not be able to think like you, either.'

'It is just you and me here. Together we will wait and see what will happen. As I told you, Your Exalted Person, when and wherever, if the word comes to me to speak, I will speak. I will tell them the truth. All the rest is up to them and their understanding and beliefs.'

With those words of mine as if the truth was only his, as if I was jealous of his truth, as if I had my eyes on his truth, and intend to take it from him, God said threateningly:

'What truth are you going to tell them?'

'I am going to tell them the truth about what you told me now, Your Honour.'

God got really angry this time.

'I will build a big and tall wall of my words between you and them. I will ensure that they will not believe you. I will darken the divine glory on your face in front of their eyes. And from now on, I order: Knowledge and thoughts like yours are sinful. I will make this an order. I will make it a rule and a contract for them. And this divine command and contract is in place from now on.'

With the words of contract and order in place, he touched the stone next to him angrily and stood up. The strength and power from his touch made seven fracture lines in the holy stone.

When the Great Commander, named Ahriman by God, tells about how His Excellency God touched the stone, it was as if a hidden power hit my face, so I got stars in my eyes, and I felt a pain like my heart had broken in seven pieces in my chest. I think the His Greatness Commander Ahriman sees the state I am in and says:

'If you want, let us go, and I will show you that holy stone. And I will tell you the end part of the story there.'

'I will always be grateful and owe to you all this knowledge, Your Greatness Commander Ahriman,' I say. 'I will never be able to pay you back.'

When Ahriman gets up slowly, I realise that he is wearing a long robe. It is of a thin, silky material that stretches down to the ground. The colour is like the smoke from tobacco, a tobacco that lights by itself. The long robe appears to be wreathed in smoke, and the smoke is surrounding his body and taking his body shape. He is slightly taller than I am. He has the long stick in his hand, the stick he was stirring the fire with, and he starts to walk in front of me. I follow Ahriman to see the stone that has the imprint of God's hand. In other words, for the sake of God's hand imprint, I follow Satan.

We go out of Ahriman's house through a different door. I say out, but I am not sure. Maybe we go in somewhere else. We come to a courtyard. The trees, the flowers, and the grass are not familiar to me, which makes me think that the garden doesn't exist on the earth or in the sky. But I know the people in the garden from their white clothes and those half-naked girls. It is those virgin girls and boys from ehl-î-malê who got here after the ceremony. They have come here to know each other, to smell each other, to be together in order to multiply.

When Ahriman and I walk past them in the courtyard, I see them close up. They are half-naked and are half-caste. They have an identifiable skin colour. Ahriman tells me that their fathers are worldly and their mothers are celestial or vice versa. According to Ahriman, that is the reason they are called ehl-î-malê. We walk past ehl-î-malê and come to a stream. The water is clear. The white and black gravel shows that the water is as deep as the measure of a hand plus a few fingers. When Ahriman lifts his robe and gets into water, I see his feet. They don't look like the hooves of a he-goat, nor do they look like talons of a falcon. I do as Ahriman does. I fold my trousers up and walk into the water.

On the other side of the stream, there is a stone, as big as the well-known watermelon from city of Diyarbekir, and in the shape of a heart. It is not black like a Hecer ul Eswed stone. It is white. It is a Hecer ul Ebyez. It looks like a holy person's headstone. I do not count the cracks, but I believe that the stone has the seven cracks that Satan Ahriman spoke of. The cracks are in purple colours and look like the veins on a clean, pure heart.

Ahriman bows in front of the Hecer ul Ebyez stone, rubs his forehead on it, and then draws back and looks at me as if to say it is my turn now. I do the same as Satan. I bow to the ground in front of Hecer ul Ebyez, put both my hands on the stone, and rub my forehead on that holy stone, the stone that has cracked in seven places from the divine wrath of God.

When I place my forehead against the stone, I feel that it is a little bit cold. It is like the coldness from the body of a snake spreading across my forehead. I don't remember any other feelings or how long I stayed like that.

When Ahriman touches my shoulder to indicate that I should get up, I realise that there is already a party going on. The melody of the harp spreads through the courtyard. Heavenly fairies and the virgins from ehl-î-malê are all mixed together. Their clean and soft bodies are twisting, curling around each other like snakes. They rejoice with each other and they become one. Their fingers and wrists look like those of Lady Leyla[32] from Botan region. The thighs and bellies resemble those of lady Salome from Samaria[33], and the swaying movements of reminds of the charmful Rachel. It seems that they all originated from this place.[34] The melody of the music and the swaying movements of

---

[32] Lady Leyla: A Kurdish princess, Leyla Bedirxan, who became a legend in the West with her dances. She was well-known especially in France for her magnificent dances. She was daughter to Sir Abdulrezak from the Bedirxan tribe in the Botan region. Among all her ballet dances, she had a well-known snake dance called Serpentine.

[33] The woman has a daughter from her ex-husband called Salome who is a famous dancer. While dancing the 'seven layer dance' at Herodes's birthday party, she removes the seven layers one by one, which makes enchants Herodes (intoxicates him with desire?). He tells her to wish anything from him. Incited (provoked, stirred) by her mother, she asks for the head of Yuhannes the Baptist. Her wish comes true. For the exchange of her beautiful, magnificent dance, she is handed the head of Yuhannes on a silver tray. Mark 6 21-29

[34] The well-known belly dancer Rachel Brice.

their soft bodies make me feel a magical wind blowing – a magical wind that enchanted Herod.[35]

At that moment, I realise that the place I have called a garden or courtyard is in fact a corner of heaven itself. The angels with thin wings, the half-naked fairies, the virgins from ehl-î-malê, streams and waterfalls with clear water, trees and exotic plants with beautiful flowers, peacocks and other birds of paradise, the melody from the harp and lute …

I am so enchanted that I imagine telling everyone in the world about everything I have seen when I return home. Whilst still in this state of ecstasy, I see that Ahriman is pointing to the white holy stone, which I identified as being from from Hecer ul Ebyez.

'Here – right here,' he says, 'we sat and started arguing. His Excellency God got angry, touched the stone with his hand and left me. To return to the story: From that day, when he hit this stone in fury, the problem started. Knowledge and thinking became sinful, and hence everything became sinful. As a matter of fact, everything happened after that day.'

---

[35] Herodes Antipas: A tetrarch who ruled Galilee and Perea. He slept with his sister-in-law (his brother's wife). Baptist Yuhannes didn't agree with that and called it a crime (sin). That makes the woman hate the Baptist.

I listen quietly. I listen to how sin was born from that day. When His Excellency Ahriman realises that I am all attention, he continues.

◆

Everyone knows what happened after that day (Ahriman says). To test his creations and his work, to prevent them from obtaining knowledge, or, in God's words, 'to stop them from sinful actions', he put the first prohibition to knowledge by saying to Adam and Eve: 'Don't eat the fruits of this tree.' That was the only prohibition so far. But it didn't work. God wanted to show his power and to show his greatness, but it didn't happen as His Excellency God wanted. Things happened as I had warned him. Both of the human beings ate the fruits of the prohibited tree, the tree of the knowledge of good and evil. "And their eyes were open and they were concious that they had no clothing."[36] Not only were their eyes opened, their thoughts became independent, and they became wiser and realised that they were naked. Let me speak clearly: human beings were not

---

[36] Bible: Genesis 3:7

aware of the thing between their legs until the day they stopped obeying him. When God saw that his imperfect creations didn't listen to him, he blamed me for it. God blamed me for his own crime and named me with anger, as if he was presenting me with a title: the Great Sinner. From then on that would be my name.

After that, God saw that human beings he created from soil did not obey his rules and they would not be corrected, and he got very annoyed. "And the Lord had sorrow because he had made man on the earth, and grief was in his heart."[37] He rued, he got hurt, he got annoyed, and he got angry. His anger grew mighty and caused all the divine works and wonders he created to be washed away in what was called the flood. Everything except for a few humans and living creatures got drowned. Those humans and animals that survived the violent rainstorm rooted themselves again and started to multiply and grow. They started their lives again. But God did not give up his habit of prohibition. He made the list of his prohibitions bigger and raised the number to ten.

For the sake of the security and to have a successful result of his divine work and magical wonders, he engraved those ten rules in stone, turned them into books, and handed them to his prophets. He put his words in the mouths of sheiks and saints. He placed his words in prophets' hands in the form of diseases, arrows, swords, fire, and death and spread them all over the universe. He continued to go his own way. He wouldn't listen to me.

When, despite all that pain and torment, he didn't get his own way, when he couldn't make head or tail of it, he got

---

[37] Bible: Genesis 6:6

offended, distanced himself from everything, and turned his back on the world. I think he was sulky because he told me: 'I will never come down to the earth. I swear on my name, I will never come down as God anymore. I leave everything to you and them, the sons and daughters of Adam and their beliefs.'

And he never came down again as God. Yes, he did get hurt from time to time when human beings did not obey his rules. I got very sad for the sons and daughters of Adam going through all the troubles and pain and being abandoned. From that day, God ordered human beings to damn me via prophets, through books, on altars, in temples, and in all languages in the world except in *Kurmandji*.[38] He was determined to make me a sinner so that he could try and test all his works and wonders.

But he got lost in the labyrinth he had built for me. He fell into the hole he had dug for me, and he is still in there. He cannot get out.

So that is the true story. The story the sons and daughters of Adam live with, the story that they believe, the story they are fooled with, the story they shed blood and they kill each other for.

---

[38] Kurmandji: A dialect or accent of the Kurdish language. Yezidi is a belief among Yezidi Kurds that forbids the word Satan. People who advocate the Yezidi belief do not use the word Satan in a good or bad way. There is no word for a malediction, damnation, or cursing in their language. The holy book for Yezidi people is called Mishefa Reş, which means The Black Book. It is written in Kurmandji dialect.

His Greatness Commander Ahriman becomes quiet after he tells the story about God and himself. I realise that it all happened because of a mistake done at the beginning. That mistake later turned into a misunderstanding that caused a war between them. It is not up to me to take sides in the matter, so I keep quiet. I understand now that to be great is an ancient malady. I want Ahriman to continue to tell me the truth of the story, for I know he has not reached the end.

So I ask him: 'OK so far, but where are your prophets, your work, your wonders, your temples, your altars, your houses, and your supporters?'

'I donated everything to God as a concession. I granted everything to him as his privilege. Human beings may not believe me, but the last wind is the witness to us. When God and I were talking and arguing here, and whether we agreed or not, I cannot remember, the last wind was blowing around us. I stood up and trapped the last wind in the North Cave and it is still in there to this day. On the last day I will open the North Cave and release the last wind all over the world so that everyone and everything will better understand the truth about me and the Lord.

'From the first day, I told the Lord the truth, opened the way for the truth, and insisted on the truth. I did not set boundaries on anyone's wishes, lusts, or desire. That is the story, and that is the truth.

'And when the first drop of blood touched the ground with the stone thrown by Cain, I knew that it would never get cleaned up and that it would never stop. All I have predicted and have told God has happened. Fights, wars, killings, pain, cruelty, suffering, and floods all followed. One after the other, all my predictions came true.

'Starting with the first drop of blood from Abel's head, sons and daughters of Adam started quarrelling. They became sworn enemies, followed by greater intensity of killings, deaths, pain, and suffering. Lies, frauds, deceit, and subterfuge spread all over like a disease. The sons and daughters of Adam have been living with all that, are still living with it, and will be living with it always.'

'Till when?' I cry, and I shock myself by the suddenness of my question. I don't know myself how it happened.

'Till the Last Day,' the Great Commander Ahriman replies.

As if right now were the Last Day, I become very quiet. I realise that the matter is bigger and more complicated than I thought. It cannot be limited to the five pillars. I understand better that the sound of the church bells and Bilali Hebeşî[39] have not reached anywhere. I feel terribly hopeless, I feel disappointed, and I feel broken-hearted. I cannot see any light or any hope. That is how I feel in front of Ahriman.

He must see how I feel. God knows that is why he looks into my eyes when he talks to me. But I cannot tell whether he is happy or sad. I want him to give me some hope, to show me a way out, to tell me as a listener to the story what to do. In other words, I want him to give me some work and targets. I want him to guide me how I can help His Greatness Commander Ahriman prove that he is not the greatest sinner.

Instead of answering my wishes and guiding me, he says:

---

[39] Belal Abyssinians – Bilal from Habes, and is considered as the firs muezzin, chosen by Prophet Muhammad himself.

'You asked me about existence and creation, and I told you the truth of the story. Up to now, none of the sons and daughters of Adam except the religious savants has been able to explain from where the sins have appeared and how they have been involved in them. But even those religious savants wove words together and made stories of them, stories that are based on lies from the start to finish because the sons and daughters of Adam love stories.'

I don't know why, but his words remind me of a Chinese saying: 'A written lie becomes truer than an unwritten truth'. Maybe that is why I tell him confidently:

'I am going to make a book out of your telling, Your Exalted Person.'

As if my words are no different from all the work, wonders, words, and rules of God – words that did not convince him and with which he didn't agree – Ahriman lifts his hands up and says:

'All you will be doing is to add one more book to the existing ones and nothing else.'

He starts walking with calm steps in front of me.

I think that he is going to show me something else in the courtyard. We walk away from the Hecer ul Ebyez stone, walk through the courtyard, and stop in front of a big gate to outside. Like a polite Kurdish gentleman, a person of refined manners, he accompanies me to the other side. I know that this is the end of the visit. I realise that I will not see him again. I feel melancholy. I don't know why, but I turn my face to the sky. At that moment I see the morning star, which seems to be coming down from the sky.

I turn sadly to Ahriman and say:

'Why did you do that to yourself? Why did you get in disagreement for the sake of the sons and daughters of Adam and get rid of your high seat up there? Why did you accept the names of sinner and loser?'

Ahriman looks at me with the same warm and friendly expression and says:

'There are victories and high places I feel ashamed of, and I feel uneasy in my name and soul for being there. And there are sins and defeats I feel proud of. Regarding the story of God and me, I choose the latter.'

One can read victory in his words and his behaviour. I am curious, I wonder and ask if he and the Lord have seen each other and have talked about the general condition from sons and daughters of Adam and about life since the last meeting at the white stone.

Yes (he says), I went myself. I went up to enter the presence of the Lord and asked him to consider coming down once more. I told him that human beings are tormenting each other a lot. I wanted him to come down and see for himself how the sons and daughters of Adam are tyrannizing and destroying each other, to see the fighting, killing, illnesses, deaths, rapes, forced marriages, birth of handicapped and blind children, and all the rest. All this is his fault. He is the responsible sinner of everything.

But the Lord still went his own way and said: 'Everything that happens on the earth, all the things human beings are going through, is all to explain my existence, my wonders. I see everything – all the suffering. I witness everything from up here. But I told you before that I am not coming down again, not as God – never!'

I replied, 'Amentubillah! Of course the Lord can see everything from up here, but it is not the same to see or to live the pain, to feel the pain with a human soul. My Lord would understand, would feel the pain better, if you came down once as a human.'

I think he was provoked by my words, for he became angry.

'OK, I will come down wherever you want and in a soul of any human you wish.'

I realise that he gets angrier quicker now than he used to.

'Come down to your Holy Land. Come down as one of your chosen servants, as Jesus, the son of Maria,' I said.

We agreed. The Lord and I agreed about something for the first time since the creation of the sons and daughters of Adam.

However, he came down to Galilee, not as God, but as one of the human beings. He transformed himself into the son of Mary, Jesus of Nazareth, and became the Messiah. He was captured by Pilate's swashbuckling soldiers at the olive mountain on the seventh day of the month. He was taken to the Sanhedrin court. Pontius Pilate asked him to tell the truth, to say who he was. Pilate made him aware that he could forgive him or he could give the order to kill him if he wished because he had the power to do so. But the Lord was stubborn then as well. He told Pilate: Don't forget: 'You would have no power at all over me if it was not given to you by God; so that he who gave me up to you has the greater sin.'[40]

---

[40] New testament / John 19:11

Without doubt it was me the Lord was aiming at because I persuaded him to come down, and he then got imprisoned by Pilate. So I was blamed for the biggest sin again. But until now, no one has known the truth about this. The Sanhedrin jury made their decision. They put a crown made of thorns from an oleaster tree on his head, laid a cross on his back, and made him walk like a sheep to be sacrificed, accompanied by insults, spitting, and whipping. They led him like a sheep for sacrifice.

In front of the gate of Jerusalem, outside the city walls, in Golgotha, he was nailed to the cross like a counterfeiter, like a sinner, by two pillager rebels. Everyone and everything witnessed the pain. Everyone and everything felt that pain. But not then and not now does anyone know why. No one understands why and how it could happen except the Lord God. Only he knows his own story. When they placed him on the cross, nailed his hands and feet, and lifted him, he turned to me and repeated his usual words:

'You made the human beings I created rebellious, and now you have tricked me.'

I felt sorry for him from my heart and the state he was in because he still wasn't aware that he is the biggest sinner.

When the Lord had his share of the pain and suffering under burning midday sun in the Golgotha square, I turned my face from him, I turned my back on him, and I walked away towards the north. I walked away from him, from his cross and from his suffering. I didn't want to see his face like that. I heard his voice behind me, and that was the last time I heard him. It was a sentence of four words of which I lost the first two, but the last two words were:

"*lama sabachtani?*"[41] But as I said, I did not return to him to answer him. I did not answer God.

———◆———

Here the Great Commander Ahriman stops talking about himself and God. He doesn't tell what happened after or how the story ended. I think maybe he just doesn't want to talk anymore, so I don't ask him when God went up to the sky from his grave. At that moment, I feel that no one really knows about his fate.

I sense that the time has arrived for me to leave and continue my journey. Still deep in thought, Ahriman turns to me.

'It is waiting for you. My black horse is waiting for you. Jump on the back of the horse and ride. Get on the road and keep going. On the way, in any places you pass through – no matter where – if you exchange words with anyone, make sure you have a chance to say your piece, too. You tell everyone without being ashamed, without being scared, without a book. When you tell the story, your inside and your outside must become one. Your heart and your mouth must become one. You and the person you are telling the story to must become one.'

I don't remember how long I stayed in the Great Commander's house and garden. When saying farewell, he told me that he had not had a visitor like me since the time of the fire. I am the first one to visit this holy land with such excitement, with such curiosity, with such a desire to know.

---

[41] The New testament/Mark 15:34 'lama sabachtani' means 'why did you leave me?' or 'why did you abandon me?' But the whole sentence is 'Eloi, eloi, lama sabachtani?' which means, 'God! God! Why did you abandon me?'

He adds: 'But, on the foundation of love and desire you have, it is impossible to build any houses, impossible to make any wealth or to bring up children.'

His words make me ponder. I try to understand what he means by building houses, making wealth, or bringing up children based on the love and desire I have. Without any attempt to solve this riddle, I bow respectfully in his presence, take my farewell, and leave the garden through the big gate.

Outside the gate, Derpiro is waiting for me, holding the reins of the soot-black horse. I realise now that the horse I was riding on to get here is the horse of the Great Commander Satan Ahriman. Once again the horse cannot stand still. He starts chewing on the bridle, scratching and scrabbling, and the steam that comes out of his funnel-like nostrils when he breathes out rises up in the nippy morning air. Derpiro hands me the reins. I jump on the back of the soot-black horse and ride away without looking back.

I am on the road. I am on the back of the soot-black horse, the horse of Satan. I am the rider of Ahriman's horse. Above my head, there is a colourful, clear sky, and in front of me there is a big, wide meadow and a long road ahead. I start urging the horse to gallop. Once again, he arches his head back towards my chest, and the smell of his sweat hits my face and makes me feel dizzy. The wind created by his speed forces me to close my eyes. It doesn't let me keep my eyelids open. The beat of the horse's hooves sounds like a tambourine in my ears. I surrender myself to its melody and to the wind.

I don't know how many dawns and dusks have passed me during this galloping journey. Nor do I know what stage of this journey I am on or where I am.

Now I start feeling warmth. I hear some voices. I force my eyelids to open. I open my ears to the voices. I wait, I think, and I try to work out where the sound is coming from.

The voice is next to me. My eyes are closed, and I don't open them. I perceive that I am lying next to a fire. I don't know how long I have been here, but I slowly come round. Lulu Khan and Lady Geshtina are asking me questions and trying to find out what has happened.

Gradually, all the events that you readers are already aware of become clearer to me. They are talking about my head injury. I feel pain in my head and realise that it has been bleeding. But I keep my eyelids very tight, and I padlock my tongue and mouth because I don't want to tell. I want everything that has happened to remain a secret between God and me. I don't want anyone to know about it. As I lay there quietly, they start to try to explain and comment on what might have happened to me. I hear them clearly now.

'Didn't you see what happened?'

'All I saw was that he suddenly fell down and remained motionless in front of the big stone.'

'God knows, he may have fainted and knocked his head on the stone.'

'But when I ran up to him, he had a stone as big as a *çortan*[42] in his hand.'

Lulu Khan, Lady Geshtina, and their two children are standing around me, and they are all talking at once. One says, 'He has hit his head on the stone,' and another one says, 'He got hit by a stone.' They throw cold water on my face and they break onion with their fists and place it under my nose, trying to wake me up with its strong smell. As I said, my eyelids are closed, but I hear everything they say. I even wrinkle my nose from the strong smell of the onion. But I keep quiet because I don't want to tell them about hitting my head, and I want everything to stay as a secret between me and God.

In order to avoid their questions, I keep my eyelids tight and stay very still. But once – only once – I open my eyes slightly and peep at them. Lulu Khan and Lady Geshtina are sitting on each side of me, and their children are standing by the top of my head. Nagina looks the same. She still has her chiffon dress on, and she is not naked. When I see Nagina, whose other magical and secret name is Demora, I feel strange. It feels as if we have known each other and been lovers for long time. I get an inappropriately timed divine wish and desire to leap up and shout her name. I want to get up, embrace her, and cry: 'Thanks for this moment! Thank God you are alive!' But I don't, not because I don't want to, but because I cannot. I know my mind and myself too well, and it will not let me do that.

---

[42] Curd or cheese made out of yogurt. The water is drained out of yogurt, and the very thick yogurt is rolled into small ball shapes and dried in the sun to be reused in the winter.

I am still lying in front of the fire with closed eyes, and I still don't want to talk. I escape into deep thoughts about everything that has happened, things that only God and I know. I talk to myself in my head: 'Behram … Behram from the land of sins, from the land of Kawash, you who started your life journey worshipping God and came all the way until now, you who studied at the school of theology to come closer to God: You have been defeated by the desires of flesh. You committed sin. You coveted a naked virgin girl. You longed to possess her. You ran off the rails from the right to the wrong, and your spirit of concupiscence overcame you. Such crimes are not forgivable anywhere, not in the front of the church gates, not in the courtyards of mosques, not in the monasteries of monks, nor in the presence of the Yezidi dervishes.

'Now, lying here in front of the fire, you cannot open your eyes from the shame of your criminal actions. You cannot look your friends in the face, and you don't want to tell the truth. Now tell me, how are you going to enter the presence of God and hide your desire of flesh from the reality? You may hide your story from your host family, you may hide it from everyone, and you may trick the prophets, but you and I – both of us know the truth about the story. We know what and how it happened. Because you are Behram and I am your desire of the flesh. You and I cannot lie to each other or trick each other. You had bad thoughts about your landlord's daughter, Nagina, and you coveted her and made yourself a sinner. You listened to the spirit of concupiscence, and you rode on Satan's donkey. You headed for the sinful roads. You travelled all the way to get an audience with Satan. You listened to him, his advice, and his doctrines. That is the whole truth, and there is no excuse. What do you say?'

I know the truth. The truth is what I am experiencing now, the situation I am in at the moment; the war, the fight that is going on in my head; a fight between me and my spirit of concupiscence, between me and the other me. It is as if I also have done like God, as if I also have created a copy of myself and the war is between me, and my spirit inside my copy.

So my heart is divided, first in two pieces, then into three pieces. One side of my heart says all this is the sorcery of this land. The second side of my heart says it is the weakness of my fleshly desires. And the third part of my heart says it is the divine wisdom of God, or else it is a joke of Satan. The last conjecture sounds more logical to me. God knows, maybe that is why I keep my eyes closed. I have drawn a blanket of silence over my head, and I am wondering how to get out of this, what and how to explain to my landlords. To escape from this situation I call to God in my heart: 'Please, God, please stretch out your hand so that goodness and righteousness will prevail.'

I feel that the hands of help are reaching me now. Lulu Khan and Lady Geshtina are wiping the blood from the wound on my forehead and bandaging it with a soft cloth. Because I can't see the wound, I don't know how deep or serious it is, but my head feels like a winter pumpkin with the cloth they wrap around it. They feed the autumn fire. I lie in front of the furnace, doze off for a while, and then come round again. I am now clear about where I am and what happened to me. I know the whole story, though I don't know how long it took and when it happened. I feel that Lulu Khan and Lady Geshtina are still sitting by my head, but the children have gone back to their chores. I can tell that from their voices.

Thinking of the wound on my head and the story I have been experiencing makes me feel hot. A fever like malaria takes over my body. I start shivering. I turn my face to the fire burning under the cauldron to avoid facing my landlords. I don't want them to ask me anything. I want to be somewhere far away, somewhere else. This is the last place I want to be at this moment. A calming heat spreads all over my face and chest from the fire. I move closer to it. The flames curl up and swirl around each other like snakes, creating multi-coloured patterns. It looks amazing.

While lying in front of the holy fire, before falling into deep thought about the story that has become a part of me, which I don't want to tell anyone, I ask Lady Geshtina for a bowl of water. I don't ask as a guest or as a wounded person. I ask in a voice of guilt and take the bowl as a sinner from her hands. I drink all the water as if the water is going to clean all my sins inside me, as if I want to wash all the sins away. I pour it all down my throat as if it is the last water I will ever drink.

When, from habit, I try to pour the last few drops left in the bowl onto the fire, my hand holding the bowl hovers over the fire like a spade hanging on the fire, and my eyes open wide. I see a hand stretching out from the fire, hindering me from pouring those last few drops of water onto the fire.

An unknown voice intones: 'Don't you know that it is a sin to put out the fire?'

The mystical voice imparts a divine fear, and I start shaking. I try to get up, but I fall back with the bowl in my hand. I try to get up again, but again I fall to the ground. I start shaking and fluttering. The sound doesn't feel strange. It is familiar, but at that moment I cannot say who it is. God knows, either it is the voice of Ahriman or Mekrus effendi, or it is the voice of both of them, I don't know. With that suspicion, taut with fear, I remember those divine words again: 'I will not hide anything inside myself. I will not steal anything from anything. I will answer all the fears and questions without being ashamed, without looking into any books. When answering, my inside and outside must become one, my heart and mouth must become one so that I and the soul in front of me can become one.'

I am aware of what is going on. Lulu Khan and Lady Geshtina are throwing themselves over me in panic. They lift me up, help me to sit, and then seat themselves beside me. Lady Geshtina starts slapping her knees to show excessive sorrow that I, Behram, have hurt myself.

'Behram, what happened to you? Poor boy! What is happening to you?'

What can I tell them? What can I do at that moment? I don't know why, but I cannot take my staring eyes from the fire. It is as if the fire has taken all my strength and energy. I feel like an empty sack. I feel numb. I am pale, I am out of strength, and I feel very dry as if all liquid has been squeezed out of my body. I manage to place myself beside the fire with the help of Lulu Khan, and nothing comes out of my mouth except the word amentubillah. This is not because of any religious belief. It is simply a reflex. The word amentubillah vibrates and breaks into pieces of voices. Even I can hear that now, sometimes loud, sometimes very quiet as if it is a secret I am telling, or something that I am ashamed of. As if I want to hide this shame, I cover my face with my hands and stay like that.

I stay like that for the time it takes to brew up a cup of tea. Then everything turns back to normal again. I become aware of everything around me – the fire and the furnace. And I want to start with my story. I swear that if it wasn't for His Excellency Ahriman and Mekrus effendi, who gave me courage, I would not be able to tell it. Now I am certain that I must tell the story which you already know. I need to tell this story without feeling ashamed, without hiding any details, without changing anything – like the Holy Writ because I know that if I don't do this, they will not leave me alone. Yes, if I hide the truth and don't tell anyone, His Excellency Ahriman and Mekrus effendi will not leave me alone. Therefore, I do it. I look at Lulu Khan and Lady Geshtina, I think very carefully and I decide that I will tell the story first to them. In other words, I tell them the story of my fate and their fate.

'I ask you in the name of God, in the name of His Excellency Ahriman, in the name of Mekrus effendi, and in the name of all the divine powers to listen carefully to my words. I … we went to the other side, Lulu Khan. Nagina and I, we went together. She led me, and we went together. First, I need to tell you that her real name is Demora … Yes, Demora and I, we went to the other side, Lady Geshtina. I met Mekrus effendi, your deceased father. I talked to his exalted person – to Mekrus effendi. I wandered around with him, and he told me Demora's name. I ask you not to doubt anything and not to fear anything. Just let me relate my story, listen until I reach the end. I will tell you each event, one by one, the things I saw, what I experienced. Mekrus effendi gave me this divine duty, and I promised to tell you. I will open my heart to you and tell everything without shame, without hiding anything. Just a few minutes ago, he made himself visible only to me and asked me again to tell you the story. I will relate everything in detail for the divine soul and wishes of Mekrus effendi.

'After coming back from the caves, I came and sat in the rock. I saw Nagina. She was naked in the pool. At that moment, I caught sin like an illness, which invaded my soul and body. God left me, and Nagina walked towards me, still naked. I did what I remember and what I could do at that moment: I bent down to pick up something. I don't remember now what it was I got and what I did with it, only that I fell down. That is all. I realised I was thirsty while lying there, so I asked Nagina for water. She then started ahead of me, and I followed her.'

As I relate the story of my journey with Nagina, I see various expressions flit across their faces – shame, curiosity, fear, happiness. I see all this emotions on their faces and in their souls, and I realise that I don't have any of those emotions left in myself. I tell everything uncovered and openly.

Lady Geshtina says anxiously, 'Because of your clean heart, my father's soul has appeared to you.'

'No,' I say. 'I went. I went myself to his place – to his dervish convent. Nagina led me, and we went together to visit him. We travelled a long way, Nagina and I, but as I said, her real name is Demora. Mekrus effendi told me. He said, "You have named her Nagina and you call her by that name, but her real name is Demora."'

After those words of mine, I see fear and worry appear on Lady Geshtina's face. She turns to Lulu Khan with that expression and says: 'I don't know if you remember Nagina's childhood, Lulu Khan. When she started talking, she used to say: "My name is Demora!" Many times she would throw herself on the floor and cry because we didn't call her Demora.'

Lulu Khan doesn't answer his wife but lowers his head and looks thoughtful. The words of his wife make me fear the truth as well. Lady Geshtina turns to me with the same worried look mixed with curiosity as if she wants me to tell more about the story of my journey and the meeting with her deceased father's soul.

'And yes,' I say, 'under the Crataegus tree, after Nagina had disappeared, after asking and begging him, he made me sacred, and I became one of the ehl-î-malê. He described the features of the ehl-î-malê and said: "The children of the ehl-î-malê are spotted between their thighs when they are young. Their death will be caused either by fire or by snake venom." Those are the very words of dear deceased Mekrus effendi, and it is my duty to tell you. I swear that all the things I tell you are true. Indeed, he told me all these things. You may think that I am crazy, that I have lost my mind, been tricked, or that I have been fooled by demons. That is not the case, Lady Geshtina. Believe me; I have experienced all the things I have told you.'

With head bent, Lulu Khan regards me silently under puckered eyebrows. God knows, he still is having doubts about the things I am saying and about the change in me. I can see that Lady Geshtina has not been thinking about the spots between the children's thighs or whether she ever tried to see if they were spotted or not when they were young. But the news that her children's death will be from fire or snake venom seems to worry her. She doesn't like the word *death* but soon calms down. Maybe she thinks that deaths that have been decided from the beginning must be down to spiritual powers, which makes her feel calmer.

As I talk, at times, I feel very light in my soul, and at times I feel very heavy. But I still tell them everything I saw and experienced in detail: the nakedness of Nagina, the height of the mountains, the moon shining on the lakes, the advice and guidance of Mekrus effendi, the ceremony of ehl-î-malê, the meeting with the Great Commander Ahriman. I tell everything. I tell them about Mekrus effendi and his cross. I tell them that God and the prophets have not been helping Mekrus effendi.

Lulu Khan and Lady Geshtina are completely silent. There is no sound coming from either of them. They don't answer any of my questions, and they don't ask any questions either. When I have finished the whole story, I see that their behaviour towards me has changed. They have their doubts about me. They are looking at me with suspicion. They must think I am a sorcerer or crazy, or a representative of spiritual souls. The truth is that I am none of these. I not a sorcerer, nor am I someone representing spiritual souls. To make them believe me – to convince them about the truth of my story – I stand up, take my shoes off, and show them the soles of my feet. I see myself that my soles and my toes are all red and swollen like bread baked in tandoori from the long journey.

Seeing the condition of my feet, I truly believe that my story is not a dream. It is a real event and the truth that I have been experiencing.

I don't remember other details of my visit, only that evening and that night. The next morning, when the darkness left and gave place to the light that woke me from sleep, I returned to the city. I don't know how I took farewell from my landlords. I cannot remember if I saw Nagina or not, but I remember well that I did not take grapes or figs with me to the city.

In the city, in my room, I am still limping because of my swollen soles and toes. The wound on my head is still fresh. I take my clothes off to wash my body without making my head wet as the wound is still fresh, not healed. Suddenly I happen to see the spots between my thighs. My privates have gone spotty like a horse's privates.

I think that it must be down to my visit to the Holy Land and to Mekrus effendi blessing and accepting me as one of the ehl-î-malê. The image of Mekrus effendi putting his hand on my head and mumbling is still fresh in my mind, like a divine picture, when I told him my wishes and asked him for guidance under the Crataegus tree. I am quite sure that I am also one of the ehl-î-malê now. Like one of ehl-î-malê, I wander around my room, thinking and thinking about the whole thing, about the spots. Three days … yes, for exactly three days, I stay in my room and do not go out at all. Let me tell you briefly, what had happened in Lulu Khan's house during those three days.

The day after I returned, a snake bit Demora while she was picking grapes, and she couldn't even make it to the doctor. She died at once. When washing her corpse, her mother had seen the spots between her thighs. Lulu Khan's original suspicion about my story of spots and snake venom changed to a whirlpool of fear and worry.

The second day, Aryan had climbed onto a haystack and set fire to it. Before anyone nearby could reach the haystack to try to put the fire out, he had turned into coal. That is how he died. They later found a piece of paper inside his shoes that he had left under a tree nearby. On the paper, he had written, 'I did not choose my birth, I did not choose my name, and it says that you cannot choose your death. It says that this is the divine work of God. But I am going to prove God's power wrong. I have been created from the earth, but I am not going back to the earth!' Then he had climbed up to the haystack, set it alight, and had become one with the flames.

After the demise of the twins, people commented on their deaths. Some people who are good at making up stories were not aware of the holiness of this event. They put the death of Demora down to the enmity of the snake and her fate. And of Aryan they said: 'They were twins, they had grown up together. Aryan couldn't stand the loss of his sister. It drove him crazy, and that is why he took his life.'

But there is another interpretation, the truth of the truths that only you and I know, that only we who are experiencing it now know.

These events that immediately followed my tale made Lulu Khan ill. Nothing could help him. Neither the divine words of God nor the prayers of the prophets could make him say a word. In other words, he was not determined like Prophet Job. He simply closed his eyes before the first light of the third day and died. No one can comprehend it, but three members of the same family had faded away as autumn leaves within three days. Three people from the ehl-î-malê had fallen down one by one, and had followed each other and are now gone. Only Lady Geshtina survived. After all that misfortune, she left her house to look for me. Like disciples of Jesus, she set out on a journey with bare feet to search for me. She wanted to see me.

And I ... I have not told you my story yet. Let me tell you.

After returning to the city, I did not attend the school of theology any more. I had lost my belief. I had become cold to the divine words and books, so I distanced myself from the school. After those three days – the three days I stayed in my room after leaving the village – I left all my books, my belongings, and my room. I left the city of E. I left and distanced myself from the land and earth that took Nagina from me, and from the land that hid and buried her inside it. I distanced from the land that washed and cleaned my soul from religion. Not only had my thoughts changed. I also had a new soul. My life changed, and I became a different me.

From that day to this, I have never come across a place or a time that gave as much, joy and pain as the one I experienced then. With the memory of that pain and joy, it is as if something is chasing me and I am running away from it, as if I am after something and constantly looking for it. I have been since that day in that psychological condition. But I don't know what I am searching for.

I still don't know. I don't know what is pursuing me, nor do I know what I am looking for and chasing. I really don't know what those two things are. However, I am sure that the day I am able to find out what these things are, I will become a poet, a lunatic, or a prophet ... a prophet without a religion and without God because right now I hate God as much as I hate Satan, and I like Satan as much as I love God.

I understand now that when you learn about the mystery of the secret things in the world, they no longer have any meaning. Since the time of those events, joy and happiness have not been mine and no longer cross my path. There is no places or nest that can open its doors and comfort me. And wherever I go, I tell everyone about the story, about what I saw and how I saw it. I tell it word for word, down to every small detail, like a divine picture. However, not even once have my words had any effect. Not one single person has bothered to think about what I said.

As I said, it wasn't only I who saw changes in me. Others also saw and heard them. People who knew me well could see that my words, my behaviour, and my actions didn't belong to me. They believed that I had borrowed those words from someone malicious. They told me this to my face. They were hesitant and nervous to voice their thoughts, but they said: 'You travel to places and say things that are not known, that do not belong here or to any sound mind.' They told me that my place was not among them, that I should be gone.

And as you all know, I am not amongst them. I still see everything clearly, as if it was written in a book lying in front of me when I think about the event, the story. It feels as if I were reading from the divine book and telling you the story. But you tell me with fear, with suspicion, with doubt that there is no such village, no such tomb, no such house, no such family, or such person as Demora. You tell me that nothing I say has happened around here or anywhere on earth.

What can I say? I was also once like that. I was also like you. I also had my suspicions and doubts. At times I, too, would say: 'If there is a God, I know that I will lose heaven, but if there is no God, then I will lose only one life.'

But I know now. I know and I feel how rich my soul is. It is rich with joy and pain, with hope and hopelessness, with knowledge and ignorance, with goodness and badness. And I received my richness of soul from the whole journey and during my search for Demora. This divine journey with its events has made me more sinful and has added more sins to the already existing ones and laid them more heavily on my shoulders. This I know. But I swear I have more knowledge and I am wiser now. I feel that I have encountered everything except death during this journey.

And even now – even when I'm no longer one of God's dear worshippers and have no belief – I still love the tomb, the house of Lulu Khan, the journey, and Demora very much. I still don't know whether Demora also loved me at that time or not, but I loved her very much. Without shame, without any fear, I say again:

I loved her more than I loved God.

About the Author

Hesenê Metê, born in 1957, is a prominent Kurdish prose writer and novelist. He was born in Ergani near Diyarbakır in Kurdistan, called Southeastern Turkey. He has been living in Sweden since the 1980s.

He has written a number of books. Some of his works have been translated into Arabic, published in Damascus and Dubai, and into Turkish, published in Istanbul.

He has taken part in various anthologies of his short stories: in German, Swedish, Turkish, and Arabic.

Some of his short stories have been played on the stage in Istanbul seasonally.

Also by Hesenê Metê:

> *The Labyrinth of the Jinns* (a novel)
> *At the Church* (a novel)
> *Mother's Breasts* (stories)
> *Tonight and the Last Story* (stories)

Lightning Source UK Ltd.
Milton Keynes UK
UKOW05f2323300617
304465UK00001B/10/P